# Patiently**Alice**

# Books by Phyllis Reynolds Naylor

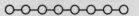

### SHILOH BOOKS
Shiloh
Shiloh Season
Saving Shiloh

### THE ALICE BOOKS

Starting with Alice
Alice in Blunderland
Lovingly Alice
The Agony of Alice
Alice in Rapture, Sort of
Reluctantly Alice
All But Alice
Alice in April
Alice In-Between
Alice the Brave

Alice in Lace
Outrageously Alice
Achingly Alice
Alice on the Outside
The Grooming of Alice
Alice Alone
Simply Alice
Patiently Alice
Including Alice
Alice on Her Way

### THE BERNIE MAGRUDER BOOKS
Bernie Magruder and the Case of the Big Stink
Bernie Magruder and the Disappearing Bodies
Bernie Magruder and the Haunted Hotel
Bernie Magruder and the Drive-thru Funeral Parlor
Bernie Magruder and the Bus Station Blowup
Bernie Magruder and the Pirate's Treasure
Bernie Magruder and the Parachute Peril
Bernie Magruder and the Bats in the Belfry

### THE CAT PACK MYSTERIES
The Grand Escape
The Healing of Texas Jake
Carlotta's Kittens
Polo's Mother

### THE WITCH BOOKS
Witch's Sister
Witch Water
The Witch Herself
The Witch's Eye
Witch Weed
The Witch Returns

**THE YORK TRILOGY**
Shadows on the Wall
Faces in the Water
Footprints at the Window

**PICTURE BOOKS**
King of the Playground
The Boy with the Helium Head
Old Sadie and the Christmas Bear
Keeping a Christmas Secret
Ducks Disappearing
I Can't Take You Anywhere
Sweet Strawberries
Please DO Feed the Bears

**BOOKS FOR YOUNG READERS**
Josie's Troubles
How Lazy Can You Get?
All Because I'm Older
Maudie in the Middle
One of the Third Grade Thonkers

**BOOKS FOR MIDDLE READERS**
Walking Through the Dark
How I Came to Be a Writer
Eddie, Incorporated
The Solomon System
The Keeper
Beetles, Lightly Toasted
The Fear Place
Being Danny's Dog
Danny's Desert Rats
Walker's Crossing

**BOOKS FOR OLDER READERS**
A String of Chances
Night Cry
The Dark of the Tunnel
The Year of the Gopher
Send No Blessings
Ice
Sang Spell
Jade Green
Blizzard's Wake

# Patiently Alice

PHYLLIS REYNOLDS NAYLOR

*alice

Simon Pulse
New York   London   Toronto   Sydney

First Simon Pulse edition October 2004

SIMON PULSE
An imprint of Simon & Schuster
Children's Publishing Division
1230 Avenue of the Americas
New York, NY 10020

Also available in an Atheneum Books for Young Readers
hardcover edition.
Designed by Sonia Chaghatzbanian
The text of this book was set in Berkeley Old Style.

Manufactured in the United States of America
10 9 8 7 6 5 4 3

The Library of Congress has cataloged the hardcover edition as follows:
Naylor, Phyllis Reynolds.
Patiently Alice / Phyllis Reynolds Naylor.—1st ed.
p. cm.
Summary: The summer after ninth grade, Alice and her friends spend three weeks working as assistant counselors at a camp for disadvantaged children and cope with all kinds of changes.
ISBN-13: 978-0-689-82636-8 (hc.)
ISBN-10: 0-689-82636-2 (hc.)
[1. Camps—Fiction. 2. Poor—Fiction. 3. Friendship—Fiction. 4. Remarriage—Fiction. 5. Family life—Fiction. 6. Single parent families—Fiction.] I. Title.
PZ7.N24 Pat 2003
[Fic]—dc21    2002012887
ISBN-13: 978-0-689-87073-6 (pbk.)
ISBN-10: 0-689-87073-6 (pbk.)

To my new Alice editor, Caitlyn Dlouhy.
Welcome.

\* \* \*

# Contents

One: Leaving Home     1

Two: Into the Wilds     21

Three: Around the Campfire     35

Four: Wet     48

Five: Gerald     63

Six: A Little Lesson in Growing Up     76

Seven: Night Out     90

Eight: News from Silver Spring     105

Nine: Going Coed     120

Ten: The Great Kelpie Hunt     131

Eleven: Girl Talk     143

Twelve: Home     155

Thirteen: Viva la Difference     167

Fourteen: The Big Announcement     179

Fifteen: The Go-Between     193

Sixteen: Confession     213

Seventeen: Celebration     224

# Patiently**Alice**

# Leaving Home

The summer between ninth and tenth grades, I learned that life doesn't always follow your agenda.

I had signed up to be an assistant counselor at a camp for disadvantaged kids. Somehow I had the idea that at the end of three weeks I could get the little girls in my cabin feeling like one big happy family. First, though, I had to talk myself into going.

I was sitting at the breakfast table watching Dad pour half-and-half in his coffee, and I decided that was a metaphor for my feelings. Half of me wanted to go to camp the following morning, and half of me wanted to stay home and be in on the excitement of Dad's marriage to Sylvia two weeks after I got back.

I wanted *some*thing to happen. I wanted at least one thing to be resolved. Everything seemed up in the air these days—Dad's engagement to Sylvia, Pamela's mother leaving the family, Elizabeth's quarrels with her parents, Lester's on-again off-again relationships with women, Patrick and I breaking up. My life in general, you might say.

"Are you eating that toast or just mauling it?" asked Lester, my twenty-something brother, who was leaving soon for his summer class at the U of Maryland. "That's the last of the bread, and if you don't want it, I do."

I slid my plate toward him. "I can't decide whether to go to camp or stay here and be helpful," I said.

"Be helpful," said Lester. "Go to camp."

I turned toward Dad, hoping he might beg me to stay.

"I can't think of a single reason why you shouldn't go, Alice," he said. "Sylvia's got everything under control."

That's what I was afraid of. Not that she shouldn't be in control. It was her wedding, not mine. But Sylvia had just got back from England, where she'd been teaching for a year, the wedding was about six weeks off, and if they had done any planning, I hadn't heard about it.

"I thought you were supposed to start planning a wedding a year in advance," I said.

"We're just having a simple ceremony for friends

and family," Dad said, turning the page of his newspaper and folding it over. He looked like a cozy teddy bear in his white summer robe with floppy sleeves, and for a moment I felt like going over and sitting in his lap. He's lost a little weight, though, on purpose. I know he wants to look handsome and svelte for the wedding, but he'll always look like a teddy bear to me.

I lifted my glass of orange juice and took a sip. "You're not just driving over to the courthouse to be married by a justice of the peace, are you?" I asked suspiciously. Maybe it was going to be even simpler than simple. I felt I couldn't stand it if Sylvia didn't wear a white gown with all the trimmings. She had already told Dad she didn't want a diamond engagement ring, and that, according to Pamela Jones, was sacrilege. "How can it be forever if you don't have a diamond?" she'd said.

"Of course we're not getting married in a courthouse," said Dad, and told me they were still planning to have the wedding at the church on Cedar Lane in Bethesda. That was perfect, because it was sort of where they'd met.

Miss Summers was my seventh-grade English teacher at the time, and—because Mom died when I was in kindergarten—I've been looking for a new mom ever since. A role model, anyway. And Sylvia, with her blue eyes and light brown hair, her wonderful smile and wonderful scent, seemed the perfect model for me and the perfect wife for Dad. All I had to do was get them together, so I'd invited her to the Messiah Sing-Along at Cedar Lane, and the rest is history.

Well, not quite. It's taken all this time to make it stick. But she finally gave up her old boyfriend, our junior high assistant principal, Jim Sorringer, for Dad. And now the wedding is set for July 28, and I wanted *details*. It had seemed impolite to start asking Sylvia questions the minute she got off the plane.

"Long gown and veil?" I asked Dad.

"No, he's wearing a suit," said Lester.

"Is *Sylvia* wearing a long dress?" I asked.

Dad smiled. "I haven't seen it yet."

"Orchestra?"

"A piano trio of a good friend of mine, Martin Small," said Dad.

"Three *pianos*?"

"Piano, violin, and cello," Dad said.

"You want him to fill out a questionnaire, Al?" Les asked. My full name is Alice Kathleen McKinley, but Dad and Lester call me Al.

"Something like that," I said, and grinned. Then I said it aloud: "I just want to feel needed, Dad. I want to make absolutely sure this wedding takes place. Maybe I ought to stay home and help out."

"If you want to feel needed, hon, you could hardly find a better place than Camp Overlook— all those kids needing attention like you wouldn't believe."

That was true, and I knew I couldn't back out anyway. Pamela Jones, Elizabeth Price, and Gwen Wheeler were going to be assistant counselors along with me. We'd been interviewed, received our instructions, gone through a day of orientation and training, and tomorrow we'd get on one of the buses taking the kids up into the Appalachian Mountains.

The phone rang for the fourth time that morning.

"I'm outta here," said Lester, scooting back from the table and picking up his books. "See you, Dad." Lester himself was looking pretty svelte these days. He has thick brown hair—on the sides, anyway. It's a little thin on top. He's taller than Dad, but I'll bet he looks a lot like Dad did when he was Lester's age. Handsome as anything. All my girlfriends are nuts about him.

I went to the phone in the hallway and picked it up. "Hello?"

"Toilet paper," came Elizabeth's voice.

"What?"

"We'd better bring our own. No telling what kind they have at camp," she said. "And tampons."

"I've already thought of that," I said. "But I still need to buy a sports bra."

"And I need a baseball cap to keep the sun out of my eyes," said Elizabeth. "You want to run over to the shops on Georgia Avenue?"

"I'll meet you outside," I said.

Elizabeth lives just across the street, and we were on our way in five minutes. We were trying to think of things we may have forgotten.

"Breath mints," said Liz.

"Mosquito repellent," I suggested.

"Imodium, in case we get the runs," she went on.

I glanced over at her, beautiful Elizabeth with her long dark hair and thick eyelashes, who was studying the list in her hand, covering every conceivable thing that might cause her embarrassment while off in the wilderness. She was wearing jeans and a white T-shirt, and was beginning to look more filled out again after a season of skinniness that had worried not only Pamela and me, but her folks as well.

"Watch out," I said, steering her away from a signpost. Gwen and Pamela and I joke sometimes that we never have to worry about anything, because Elizabeth will do our worrying for us. Which isn't exactly true, of course. We just worry about different things.

We got the bra and the cap and stopped at the drugstore for the rest. I was heading for the checkout counter with my mosquito repellent when Elizabeth called, "One more thing, Alice."

I went back to find her looking at men's hair tonic and shaving cream.

"Now what?" I asked.

"Just a minute," was all she said.

I leaned against the shelves behind me and noticed how hair products for men took only half the space of hair stuff for women. *Maybe because women have twice as much hair,* I thought, smiling to myself. I'm letting my hair grow long now. It's almost as long as Elizabeth's, but Pamela still wears hers short, and looks more sophisticated.

I was anxious to get home and finish packing, so when I saw Elizabeth moving slowly along the display a second time, I said, "What are you looking for? Let me help." Maybe she was supposed to buy something for her dad.

"Oh . . . something," said Elizabeth.

"*What?* I want to get home."

"Alice, I promised myself I wouldn't leave this store until I found them," she said. And then, looking quickly around, she whispered, "Condoms."

"*Condoms?*" I yelped. I couldn't help myself.

Elizabeth clapped one hand over my mouth, but there was no one in our aisle to hear. I jerked her hand away.

"Are you nuts?" I said. "Who for?"

*"Anyone,"* Elizabeth said determinedly. And then she added, "Well, for Pamela, mostly. Just in case."

*"Pamela?"*

"Well, you know how moody she's been lately."

"In case of *what*? She's moody so she needs condoms?"

"Her mother and everything."

"Her *mother* needs condoms?"

"Oh, Alice, when someone's as upset as Pamela, she could do all sorts of things you wouldn't expect. We don't know who she's going to meet or what the guys are like, and she'll be away from home. . . ."

"So will *we*!" I said.

"Look," she told me, "I was reading this article— 'If He *Won't*, Then *You Should*'—and it said that especially when a girl is away from home, she should have back-up protection in case she's in a situation she can't control."

I don't know where Elizabeth finds this stuff.

"If she can control it enough to get a guy to put on a condom, I'd think she could also get herself out of there," I said.

"Okay, but we *don't* know what's going to happen at camp, right?"

"Hardly *that*!" I said.

"But just in case, I'll have condoms for anyone who needs them," she told me.

I sighed. Elizabeth has been trying so hard to be cool lately that she's getting bizarre. But right then she looked like a little Mother Superior trying to protect us all, and it struck me as pretty funny.

"Maybe condoms are in the plumbing section," I said.

"What?" She turned and looked at me.

I tried not to laugh. "You know . . . you put them on a man's . . . uh . . . faucet."

She gave me a sardonic smile. "Be serious."

"Toy counter? When you want to *play*?" I suggested. "Automotive needs? In case you do it in the backseat of a car?"

"Alice!"

"How about over with the school supplies? No, I've got it! In men's wear!"

She ignored me. "I wonder if we need a prescription."

"Let's go home," I told her.

"No!"

A clerk appeared at the end of our aisle with a box of deodorants and began shelving them. I pushed Elizabeth forward. "Go ask him," I said.

The man looked up. "Can I help you?" he asked. He was a plump guy of about thirty, friendly and businesslike.

"Yes," Elizabeth said, her words coming in a

rush, cheeks pink, "I wonder if you could tell me where I could find men's condoms."

The clerk paused only a moment, then said, in the same businesslike manner, "Aisle eight, next to women's sanitary products."

Now Elizabeth's face turned crimson. The clerk immediately returned to his deodorants, and I pushed Elizabeth around the corner into the next aisle, where we collapsed against each other, trying not to laugh out loud.

"I was so *embarrassed*!" she gasped. "If anyone *heard* . . . !" And then, as though afraid she might lose her nerve, she propelled herself toward aisle eight. The next thing I knew we were standing in front of a row of little boxes, with pictures of men and women in romantic poses, walking along the beach at sunset or dancing among palm trees.

Elizabeth grabbed a box of Trojans and was off toward the cash register, her face still peppermint pink. I tagged gleefully along as she surveyed the three lines. Two of the cashiers were men in their twenties. Elizabeth took the line with a middle-aged woman at the register.

Standing behind her, I rested my chin on her shoulder. "She's probably going to ask if you have a permission slip from your mother," I whispered.

"Shut up," Elizabeth murmured.

"Maybe you have to be eighteen. Maybe she'll call the manager," I went on.

"Alice!"

We were next in line. I plunked down my mosquito repellent, and Elizabeth put down a package of breath mints, another of Imodium, and the condoms. We put our money on the counter as the woman rang up the items, but when she picked up the box of condoms, she couldn't find a price sticker. And then, while we cringed, the grandmotherly looking lady held them up and called out in a gravel-truck voice, "Frank, do you know how much these are?"

The thin-faced man at the next register said, "What are they? Regular?"

And the woman said, "No, lubricated tip."

Now both our faces were burning.

The man gave a price, the clerk rang them up, and the minute Elizabeth had the sack in her hand, we headed for the exit.

"That's another store I can never enter for the rest of my natural life," said Elizabeth.

I'd been home only ten minutes when the phone rang.

"Alice, do you have any good mysteries? I want something to read in case I'm bored out of my skull," came Pamela's voice.

"Elizabeth doesn't think that will happen," I said. "She's bringing condoms."

"*Elizabeth?*" cried Pamela.

"For you," I added.

There were three seconds of silence, and then we both burst out laughing.

"She sure must think I lead an exciting life," Pamela said.

"I think she's more afraid that you *will*!" I told her.

"Can you see Elizabeth going into a drugstore and asking for condoms? I mean, can you even imagine that?" Pamela asked me.

"Now I can," I told her. "I was there."

Sylvia came for dinner that night. "Well, are you excited, Alice?" she asked.

"Are *you* excited?" I countered. "Your wedding's next month!"

"Yes, but I'm so busy, I hardly have time to think," she said.

As soon as she had walked in, she and Dad embraced, and I looked away. I mean, it's such a private moment. I guess the other reason I look away, though, is because their kisses are reminders of Patrick and me—the way we used to kiss. And though I'm supposed to be over him now—we broke up last fall—I guess you never quite forget your first real boyfriend. It helps, of course, that we're still friends, but it's hard to think of someone as just another buddy when you've been as close as we were.

"I've got a list of things to do for each of the five weeks, and first on my list, while I can catch you, Alice, is to ask if you'll be my bridesmaid," Sylvia said. And before I could even squeal out my delight, she said, "My sister's coming from Albuquerque to be my maid of honor."

"Of course I'll be a bridesmaid!" I said. "How many are you going to have?"

"Just you and Nancy. I have so many friends at the school that if I picked any one of them, the others would get upset. So I'm going to choose only the two women closest to me."

*Women!* She had called me a *woman!* I could almost feel my breasts expanding inside my 32B bra.

"Oh, Sylvia!" I said.

"I've got a dressmaker who says she can whip up two dresses in time, and I got my gown off the rack, so if you'll choose the dress you like, I'll have it made while you're at camp," Sylvia said.

Dad and Lester were busy making beef Burgundy for dinner, so Sylvia and I took over the dining room table and she put three different dress patterns in front of me. Her color scheme, she said, was teal and royal blue. I couldn't imagine it until I saw the two colors together, and they worked really well. Her sister was going to be in royal blue, so I got to be in teal. That pleased me because my hair is strawberry blond. In some lights it looks blond, in some it looks red, and at night it even looks brown, but blue green is definitely good on me.

The gowns were all very simple in design. One was straight across the front with spaghetti straps and a long narrow skirt; one had a scoop neckline and short sleeves, and the third had a V neck with straps that crossed in back.

"I can choose any one of them?" I asked.

"Yes," said Sylvia. "Nancy's already chosen the one she likes best, but I'm not going to tell you which it is. You should have the gown you like best. I'm not one of those people who believes bridesmaids should look like identical twins."

"I like the one with the spaghetti straps," I said.

"That's exactly the one Nancy chose," she said, and hugged me. "Excellent taste, Alice. As soon as we have dinner, I'll take your measurements."

"Oh, her measurements are simple," Les said from the doorway. "Thirty . . . thirty . . . thirty."

"*Lester!*" I said.

Sylvia just laughed. "Don't you believe it, Alice. You've got a great figure."

Sylvia Summers is the only one who could ever lie and get away with it. I'm more like thirty-two, twenty-five, thirty-four, but what I was really wondering right then was if my bra and underpants had holes in them and whether I'd have to take off everything to be measured.

At the table Lester asked Sylvia, "Do you actually enjoy this? The photographer, the cake, the flowers, the rings, the candles, the music, the . . ."

"I love it," said Sylvia.

"Actually," said Dad, "we've sort of divided up the work. She's taking care of the wedding details, and I'm arranging the honeymoon."

"Sounds fair," said Les.

I was able to slip away before dinner was over and change my bra, which had old elastic in back, and by the time Sylvia came upstairs with the measuring tape, I was in my robe.

She's very efficient and acted as though this were what she did every day of her life: measured girls in their underwear. I knew I shouldn't have minded—she was almost my stepmother—but I was glad when I could put on my robe again.

"Well, someday, Alice, it will probably be you and me in a room together taking measurements for your *wedding* dress," she said, smiling.

I smiled back and said flippantly, "And having

that intimate conversation for the bride-to-be."

She laughed and I laughed, and then, because my joke had gone over so well, I took it a step further: "But now *you're* the bride, so if there's anything you need to know, Sylvia, just ask me."

"Well," she said, "nothing I can think of at the moment. Is there anything *you* would like to ask *me*?"

I could feel myself blushing. Had I been that obvious? Had she seen right through me? What I really wanted to know, of course, was whether she and Dad had already made love, but it was none of my business and I wouldn't ask it in a zillion years.

"No," I said, "but if I think of something, I will."

"Good," said Sylvia. "I want to keep things open and honest between us. I know we won't get along perfectly all the time—no one does, not even Ben and me. But I'd like it if we could promise each other that when something upsets us, we'll talk it out. There's nothing worse than people going around holding grudges and never talking about them and nobody quite knowing who's mad about what. Agree?"

"Yeah, that's pretty awful," I said, thinking of the time Elizabeth and Pamela had turned against me for a while and nobody would come right out and say what was wrong.

"Is that the way you and Dad solve problems? Talk them out?"

"We're working on it," she said.

I got one more call before I went to bed that night. It was Gwen.

"You all packed, girl?" she asked.

"All except the small stuff," I said. "You know what I wish? I wish we were going to a camp where we wouldn't need a hair dryer, conditioner, nail file, lip gloss. . . ."

"It's called Girl Scout Camp," she told me. "We've been there, done that. Those kinds of camps, I mean."

"So it's all about guys, isn't it? Who we might meet?" I said.

"You could say that," said Gwen. I thought of her perfect eyebrows, her short but shapely legs, her skin the color of cocoa. I'll bet she's had a different boyfriend for every year of her life, though she and Leo—Legs is his nickname—have been going together for eighteen months.

"So what's up?" I asked her.

"Legs and I had a fight," she said.

"You broke up?"

"Not exactly. He said he was going to drive out and visit sometime during the three weeks we're at camp, and I said I didn't want him to. I think he's been seeing another girl when I'm out of the picture, and I guess I just want to be free to fool around myself if I meet somebody."

"Fool around . . . meaning . . . ?" I asked.

She laughed. "Hang out with . . . kiss . . ."

I couldn't help myself: "Elizabeth's bringing condoms," I said.

I heard the expected gasp at the other end of the line. *"Elizabeth?"*

"For Pamela. Just in case. She says anything could happen."

She laughed. "She goes around thinking like that, anything *might*. Anyway, I just wanted to tell you that if Legs calls asking for directions to that camp, don't give them to him. Okay?"

"Got'cha," I told her.

I had just gone to bed when the last call came. Dad tapped lightly on my door. "Al? Hate to disturb you, but it's your Aunt Sally. Shall I tell her you've gone to bed, or do you want to talk with her? It's only ten o'clock Chicago time."

"I'll take it," I said groggily, and padded out to the upstairs phone in the hallway. If I didn't talk to her now, I knew she'd call again the next morning when I was trying to get out the door.

"Oh, Alice, dear, I just want to wish you a very happy time at Camp Overlook," Aunt Sally said.

She's Mom's older sister and looked after our family for a while after Mom died. She and Uncle Milt have a daughter named Carol, a few years older than Les.

"Thanks, Aunt Sally," I said. "I'm an assistant counselor, you know. I'm not going as a camper."

"I know that, dear. Counselors have a lot of responsibility, and little children look up to them."

I wondered why Aunt Sally didn't give her sermons from a pulpit every Sunday.

"Meaning . . . ?" I said, knowing very well that Aunt Sally didn't call just to wish me happy camping.

"Why, nothing, dear! I think it's wonderful that you are going to be a role model for all those little children. They'll want to imitate everything you do."

"Thank you," I said.

There was a brief silence, and then Aunt Sally said, "Your father tells me it's a coed camp."

*Here it comes,* I thought. "Yes," I told her.

"So there will be male counselors as well as female?"

"That's what 'coed' means, all right," I said.

"Well, as I said to your Uncle Milt, you're Marie's daughter, and I know you would want her to be proud of you. Of course, this is the first time you've been away from home for any length of time, and there are all those woods and hills and valleys and—"

"Aunt Sally," I interrupted, trying not to laugh, "are you afraid I'll get lost?"

"Oh, no," she said.

"Are you afraid I'll drown?"

"Not really."

"Are you afraid I'll go off in the woods in a fit of passion?"

"Why, whatever made you say that?" Aunt Sally choked.

"Because I can read you like a book," I said gently. "Actually, I doubt there's anything you could worry about that Elizabeth Price hasn't thought of first. But I appreciate your call, and I will really try to have a most magnificent summer, role model and all."

# 2

# Into the Wilds

Gwen's mother was to pick us all up the following morning. I gave Dad and Lester a hug and went over to Elizabeth's to wait.

Liz was not only looking more normal these days—she wasn't putting purple in her hair any longer—but she seemed more relaxed, if you can ever call Elizabeth relaxed. She saved her hugs and kisses for her little year-and-a-half-old brother, though—just a quick "Bye-bye" to her parents, and that must have hurt. Both Elizabeth and Pamela were having parent problems, and I was glad it was Gwen's mom driving us to the recreation center, where we would board the buses.

Pamela was with the Wheelers when they drove up, and all four of us—Gwen and Liz and Pamela and me—were in shorts and tank tops. Elizabeth's legs actually looked good again; you wouldn't mistake her for a prisoner of war, with sticklike thighs and knobby knees.

Mrs. Wheeler was on the short side, like Gwen, and wore her hair in a well-shaped Afro. "Off you go, into the wilds," she said, smiling. "Please don't break any bones, Gwen."

Gwen's mom is a lawyer who works at the Justice Department. Even though it was Saturday, she looked smart in her linen shirt and pants, while we looked like we were going to dig potatoes or something. "Your father wants you to call home every weekend," she said. I saw Gwen roll her eyes. "Humor him, please."

"And I suppose I should call Granny," Gwen said.

"That would be nice."

I think we all envied Gwen's extended family. She seemed to have aunts and uncles and cousins and grandparents all over the place. The closest relatives I've got are Dad's brothers, Uncle Howard and Uncle Harold—twins—down in Tennessee, though I don't see them as often as I see Aunt Sally in Chicago.

So one minute we were taking our bags out of the trunk of Mrs. Wheeler's car, and the next we were walking up the sidewalk toward the recreation center, where about eighty kids were milling about, yelling and chasing each other, swinging their duffel bags at friends, teasing, laughing, jumping, and spinning, all except a dozen or so who had grown tearful and were clinging to a relative or caretaker.

The full counselors were already at work comforting the weepers, and after pointing out the buses we'd be riding on, they gave us clipboards with names of campers on them. We were each responsible for locating the kids on our list and showing them where to line up.

I had just started toward a group of girls sitting on the steps of the building when I heard Pamela say, "Whoa!" Coming out the door of the center were two guys, *very* good-looking guys, also holding clipboards. They noticed us about the same time and came over.

"Name, please?" one of them said to Pamela jokingly, looking over his list. "Age? Marital status?"

We smiled.

"Craig Kimball," he said to all of us. "Nice to meet you."

"Andy Simms," said his friend, a tall African American wearing an Orioles T-shirt.

"I'm Pamela. This is Elizabeth and Alice and Gwen," Pamela told them.

"You have your cabin assignments yet?" asked Craig. "It's there on top of your clipboards."

We checked. Gwen and I discovered we were in the same cabin, number six. Elizabeth was in eight, and Pamela was in twelve.

"Darn!" said Craig. "They did it again, Andy. Girls on one side of the camp, guys on the other."

We laughed, but there were kids to be rounded up, so off we went.

Gwen and I were to be in charge of six girls, ages seven to ten. One was a little Korean girl, Kim, who sat tearfully on the steps clinging to a grown woman.

It was Gwen who knew how to handle that. She reached in her duffel bag and pulled out a little black box, the hinged kind that jewelry comes in. She simply sat down on the steps next to the little girl and, without a word, opened the box. Inside was a butterfly, perfectly preserved under a plastic bubble. Its wings were a shimmering pattern of brown and yellow with orange spots.

Gwen held it out for Kim to see.

"It's beautiful," said the woman, and introduced herself as Kim's aunt.

"Can I touch it?" asked Kim.

"No, because it would crumble," Gwen said. "I collect them. But not till after they die."

Then she let Kim try on her watch and rings, and by the time we were to get on the bus, Kim had attached herself to Gwen, and I herded the other five girls on board.

The youngest was a chubby African-American

girl of seven named Ruby, but the smallest child, who was eight, was Josephine. I swear I could have carried her about in one arm. She and her older sister, Mary, were the only white kids in the bunch. Then there was Estelle, who was Latina, and Latisha, the oldest of the six girls, also black. We decided it was no accident that each cabin was a miniature melting pot.

When we finally had our girls settled and their belongings accounted for, and Craig and Andy had done the same with their campers, our bus pulled away. Gwen looked at me and said, "Well, *our* lives are about to change!"

For the worse, it seemed, because a boy at the back of the bus started singing "Ninety-nine Bottles of Beer on the Wall," only his friend changed the lyrics to "Ninety-nine bottles of snot on the wall." As the song progressed, the word became "pee," then "poop," and each new word brought yelps of laughter from the boys and at least half the girls. The other girls covered their ears and pretended to look offended.

I glanced across the aisle at Pamela and Elizabeth and shouted, "Do you think you can stand this for three weeks?"

But Elizabeth was looking toward the front of the bus and smiling, and when I followed her gaze, I saw Craig and Andy looking back at us.

"Oh, yes!" Elizabeth said in answer. "I think I can stand this very well."

We decided that Camp Overlook must have been built for munchkins, because there were two facing rows of small cabins, twelve in all, odd numbers on one side of camp, even on the other. Each was crammed with four bunk beds but no facilities—just two small dressers with drawers, some shelves, and eight coat hooks. We'd read that it was owned by a church, which donated the camp to the county's social services for three weeks each summer to provide summer camp for poor kids. It was run on a shoestring, and none of us expected more than the basics. The basics were all we got.

Each cabin had either one counselor and seven campers or two assistant counselors and six campers. Each cabin was to choose a name for itself. Our girls chose the Coyotes, which should have told us something right there.

The first hurdle we faced was the sleeping arrangements. Mary, we discovered, did all the talking for her sister. "Josie can't sleep on the top," she announced. "She has to sleep on the bottom."

"Okay," I said. "Mary will sleep on the top bunk of this bed, and Josephine will sleep on the bottom."

Mary surveyed the sloping roof of the cabin with a wary eye. "I can't sleep on the top either because of spiders," she said, which just about cooked the top bunk for anyone else, and Gwen and I knew where *we'd* be sleeping.

But seven-year-old Ruby was our salvation. "Yeah, but if you sleep on the bottom bunk, there's bears!" she said knowingly.

"And snakes!" said Estelle.

Now everybody wanted a top bunk.

We decided at last that Gwen and I, Josephine, and Kim would all have lower beds. Mary would sleep above her sister; Ruby would sleep above me; Estelle would sleep above Kim; and Latisha would sleep above Gwen. That settled, we assigned drawers and shelf space for our belongings, and the last order of business was to confiscate every piece of candy, bag of chips, or box of cookies in or out of sight. Each child had been instructed not to bring food or anything that would attract wildlife, but as pockets and bags were inspected out fell Snickers bars, cheese twists, animal crackers, and pretzels.

Each child solemnly turned in her supply, all but Josephine, who had two Hershey's Kisses squeezed tightly in her tiny fist.

"She doesn't want to let go," said Mary, reporting the obvious.

We explained about mice and rats and raccoons and squirrels, and how we would keep all our treasures in this big metal box that came with each cabin, but Josephine's fist remained closed.

"She likes Hershey's Kisses," said Mary.

We knew this was going to be a contest of wills, and while it was important that we show who was in control, we didn't want a major scene over two Hershey's Kisses.

"Tell you what," said Gwen. "I'm going to close my eyes and hold out my hand, and when I count to three, Josephine will drop one of the kisses in my hand. Okay?"

The other girls gathered around to watch this strange proceeding. Josephine stared at Gwen out of her small, narrow face.

Gwen closed her eyes and held out her hands. "One . . . two . . . three," she said.

*Plop.* It was like magic.

"Thank you," said Gwen. "We'll just put this in the box, and you can have it after lunch. Now I'll close my eyes again and count to three, and you give me the other one. One . . . two . . . three."

Nothing happened.

"She doesn't want to do it," said Mary.

"You can have them both after lunch," said Gwen.

Josephine shook her head. The Hershey's Kiss, what was left of it, was beginning to melt in the warmth of Josie's hand, and chocolate oozed out from between her fingers.

I snuggled up close to Josephine on the bottom bunk and put my arm around her. "How about if I trade you a real, live kiss for that ooey, gooey chocolate in your hand?" I said. "Okay?"

Josephine just looked at me. I leaned over, took her face in my hands, and gave her a big fat kiss on the cheek, grinning at her. I got the chocolate, and we all set off for lunch in the dining hall. Following along behind the girls, Gwen and I gave each other a high five.

Pamela and Elizabeth were just going ahead of us with their groups when we got there, and as we went through the door I heard Pamela say, "Oh, my gosh! They're gorgeous!"

Coming through the door on the other side of the hall were Andy and Craig and a couple more guys. I don't know if it was because they were brawny and tanned (some of them, anyway) or because we were feeling rather desperate for male company, but they sure looked good to us. One of them had an acne-scarred face, but his smile was warm, he was cute, and his little charges were hanging all over him. If there's one thing that's attractive to a girl, it's a guy who seems to get along well with kids.

"I get the one in the sweatshirt," Elizabeth murmured.

"There are two in sweatshirts, Liz," Pamela said. "I want the one in the red shorts."

"That's the one I meant!" Elizabeth told her.

"Sorry, he's taken," Pamela joked.

As they directed their boys to one of the long wooden tables Craig asked us, "So what name did you pick for yourselves? Andy and I got the Buzzards."

"Coyotes," I told him.

"Bunnies," said Elizabeth.

"Mermaids," said Pamela.

"Hey, guys," Andy said to the little boys hanging on his arm. He motioned toward Pamela's girls. "Meet the Mermaids."

"Yuck!" said one of his boys, who immediately grabbed a bench at the table, spreading out his arms and legs the length of it. "Don't let the girls sit here," he warned his fellow campers, and the game was an instant success: Never let the girls sit at a boys' table. As though they would have. The Coyotes chose a table as far from the Buzzards as they could get, while the Bunnies and Mermaids all turned their backs on the boys at the next table.

"Welcome, campers!"

The camp director for Camp Overlook was not the woman who had interviewed us back home, but a short curly-haired woman in jeans and a CAMP OVERLOOK T-shirt. Connie Kendrick's voice was loud for so small a woman, but she absolutely radiated cheerfulness. You had the feeling that if the dining hall were sliding down the mountain, she would still be smiling.

"I am *so* glad to have you here for three weeks at Camp Overlook!" she said.

"And the very first thing we need to do, before we *eat,* even, which is the *next* most important thing we do, is learn the Camp Overlook cheer. And here it is:

> 'Clap your hands!
> Stamp your feet!
> Our Camp Overlook
> Can't be beat!'

"Everybody, now! Say it with me!"

The dining hall resounded with the sound of hands clapping, the wooden floor rocked with the vibration of stamping feet, and all the kids shouted the cheer together.

Then each table assigned a designated runner to go to the kitchen and return with platters of hot dogs, French Fries, sliced tomatoes and cucumbers, and large squares of chocolate brownies for dessert. The way some kids ate, I wondered if this was the first full meal they'd had that week.

"Here comes five pounds, easy!" Gwen moaned, but we were hungry already, and when we'd polished off a hot dog, we each took a brownie.

After lunch the assistant director, Jack Harrigan, introduced all the full counselors and assistant counselors. I noticed that the guy both Pamela and Elizabeth had their eyes on was Ross Mueller. The cute guy with the acne was Richard Harrigan, Jack's son. Connie Kendrick went over the camp rules, and then there was a guided tour of the whole place. This gave the assistant counselors a chance to hang back and talk with each other while the kids trooped on ahead of us, following Connie and Jack.

"So where you girls from?" Ross asked Elizabeth as we headed down to the river. He was one of the blondest guys I'd ever seen. His skin was tanned, and this made the hair on his arms and legs, his eyebrows, even, seem blonder still. Even Pamela's short hair was not as light as his.

"Silver Spring," she told him, smiling. "What about you?"

"Philly," he said.

"You came all the way here from Pennsylvania?" Pamela asked in surprise.

"Yeah. I'm going to major in P. E. Figure 'assistant counselor' will look pretty good on a college application." He grinned at her. "So what brought *you* here? The scenery? The kids? The food? The river?"

We laughed, because Camp Overlook is to camps in general what Motel 6 is to hotels, what Budget is to rental cars. No frills. Part of the riverfront was sectioned off for swimming. Next to that were a couple of rowboats and, farther on, a bunch of canoes. That was the extent of water sports.

"Not the river, that's for sure," Pamela said.

"Not the food," added Elizabeth.

"The company," said Gwen, eyeing another assistant counselor, almost as short as Gwen but probably the most muscular guy in the camp. I figured she was going to forget Legs in a hurry.

"Ah, yes! The company!" said Ross, and grinned at Elizabeth this time.

We kidded around all the way to the baseball diamond, but when Connie got to the edge of the field where the woods began, with various paths leading off into the trees, she faced the young campers. "You are *never* to go on any of these trails without the permission of your counselor, and you are never to go alone. Some of these paths go on for miles, folks. It's easy to get lost. We're going to follow one right now, though, to the overlook, for which the camp is named."

We went to the overlook then, Gwen and I elbowing each other at the way Elizabeth and Pamela were both competing for Ross's attention. Elizabeth's voice gets higher when she talks to a guy she likes, while Pamela's gets more sultry. Sophisticated Pamela acts a little too blasé, as though she could hardly care less, while Elizabeth is all enthusiasm.

"When you become a psychiatrist," Gwen whispered to me, "they're your first case study."

"Psychologist," I said. "No med school for me."

The overlook was probably the only—and certainly the most—spectacular thing about Camp Overlook. On a natural promontory, protected by a chest-high stone wall, we could see far out over the valley and the mountains beyond—layer upon layer of gray blue.

One of Andy's boys tried to climb up on the four-foot wall, and Andy was after him in a second. It wasn't a sheer drop-off—if he'd fallen, he would have rolled—but it was a lesson to all of us just how alert we had to be.

Maybe it was a good thing that the boys' cabins were on one side of the clearing and the girls' on the other, I thought as we went back to camp for quiet time. The way Pamela and Elizabeth were watching Ross, half our girls could have run off before they'd notice.

# 3

# Around the Campfire

We spent the "quiet hour" not very quiet at all, settling some disputes about whose stuff was taking more shelf space and whose sneakers were smelling up the place.

Gwen and I began to see a pattern: Ruby and Kim were the clingiest. When either of us sat down on the edge of our bunk, one or both of those girls were right beside us, leaning against us, stroking our arms, toying with our hair. Estelle was a troublemaker; Latisha, the oldest, the aloof one. Josephine was used to playing the "baby" role, with Mary, her sister, her appointed nursemaid and caretaker.

*Did I know what I was in for?* I wondered as I got up to get some Kleenex from my bag, and instantly Ruby and Kim rose up on either side like appendages and moved with me across the floor.

I could have been swimming at Mark

Stedmeister's pool. I could have been going to the movies with Lester or ordering Chinese to eat at home with Dad. But I told myself it was only three weeks out of my life, and it would give Dad and Sylvia a chance to be alone. Besides, Lester would appreciate me all the more when I got back. Maybe.

"I'm tired already," Gwen confided when the Coyotes settled down at last to trade stick-on tattoos, which most had brought along. Gwen and I simply stretched out on our bunks to rest up for whatever lay ahead. We were too tired to even sit up.

Dinner that night was chicken and noodles and a tossed salad. Josephine wouldn't eat it.

"She only eats fried chicken," Mary explained.

"Well, that's too bad, Josephine, because this is all we've got," I told her. "If you don't like the chicken, eat the noodles."

"They look like worms," said Josephine, which was about the first intelligible thing she'd said since she'd got here, and I wanted to throttle her.

"Eeuw!" said Estelle and Ruby.

"Worms!" said Latisha.

"And they're absolutely delicious. Eat!" Gwen commanded.

Everyone ate but Josephine.

The afternoon had been exhausting. After quiet time we'd had a relay race, followed by a volleyball game, followed by a swim, but most of the kids claimed the water was too cold. So the dining hall smelled not only of chicken and noodles and disinfectant, but of hot sweaty bodies and stringy hair.

"Okay, campers, listen up!" said Connie when the cherry Jell-O dessert had been served. "At Camp Overlook we take our showers *before* we go to bed, not when we get up in the morning. The sheets are changed only once a week, and we want to be kind to our bunk mates and not stink up the cabins."

All the kids laughed and pointed at each other.

"So here's the plan," Connie continued. "After dinner you are to shower, then put on your pj's. Did everyone bring pajamas as the instructions told you to do? And then I want you—softly, silently, like deer in the moonlight—to follow your counselors to the campfire." Her voice got very low. "I want you to come so quietly that, just like deer, no one will hear you coming. The others will turn around and there you are, just like that."

At first there was a lot of hooting and snickering at even the word "pajamas," because pajamas are too much like underwear, and all you have to say to this crowd is "underpants," and they practically roll on the floor in laughter. But the "silently, like deer in the moonlight" phrase made them pause, and we noticed that they were quiet already, just leaving the dining hall.

Because the showers could hold only so many girls at once, two cabins were to go at a time, and when our girls were through, we were to knock on the doors of the next two cabins till everyone had a turn. Later, after the kids were clean and back in the cabins, the counselors got to shower, half of them at a time, while the others took charge.

Once inside the wooden walls of the shower house, though, our little campers hesitated, their towels wrapped tightly around them.

"C'mon, before the water gets cold," I called, testing it with one hand. I didn't want to tell them it was barely warm to begin with. "Last one in is a rotten egg!" I couldn't help smiling to myself, because I could remember when Elizabeth and Pamela and I used that line, only then we said, "Last one in is a virgin" and felt so sophisticated!

The younger girls gave in first—Ruby, then Josephine, and finally Kim. But the older girls hung back. We noticed the same reluctance from the girls in Elizabeth's cabin. We tried to be casual about it and sat down on a bench at one end. Tommie Lohman, Elizabeth's cabin mate, was a tall thin girl with light brown hair and very long legs. She had an easy, languid way about her that gave the impression she was in no hurry to see what the next day or month or year would bring.

At last all the Coyotes and Bunnies were standing in a line under the showers, hitting the soap dispensers with the palms of their hands and lathering up, eyeing each other furtively while they scrubbed.

Gwen and Elizabeth and I were listening to Tommie's funny account of all the things she'd forgotten to bring, when suddenly Latisha yelled, "She's lookin' at me!" and pointed to a girl in Elizabeth's cabin.

"Tend to your own bathing, Marcie," Elizabeth told the freckled girl.

But a moment later Latisha complained, "Now she's lookin' at me back *there*!"

"Latisha, your body's no different from anyone else's, so cool it," Gwen said.

"What if the boys come in?" asked Estelle warily.

"The boys have their own showers on the other side of camp," I told her.

"But what if they peek?" asked Ruby.

"Then we'll dunk their heads in the toilet," said Gwen, and the girls screeched with laughter.

At some point Josephine got Ruby's washcloth by mistake, and when they traded back again,

Estelle jeered to Josie, "Ha-ha! Now you got nigger water on you!"

"Estelle!" I said, surprised, and the other girls covered their mouths in shock. They all turned to see what we would do.

"You watch your mouth, girl," Latisha warned Estelle, her eyes menacing.

*Choose your battles,* our counselor's handbook had said. *Some issues are worth addressing immediately, and some can be saved for later.* I decided not to make a big issue of it on our first night here in camp.

"I hope I won't hear that word again, Estelle," I told her. Gwen said nothing, and I knew she was waiting for the right time and place too.

When the girls were clean and back in the cabin, we counselors bathed alone, in record time. By then there was no hot water at all, and I was grateful for my flannel pajamas. It's *cold* in the mountains! Then, when the path to the showers had grown quiet, we heard a soft bell announcing the campfire. We all put on our sneakers and jackets and—just as Connie said—like deer coming out to cross the meadow in the moonlight, we walked silently out in the field, where logs had been placed in ever widening circles, and there was the smell of smoke in the air.

I had thought that this would be the highlight

of the day. I had thought that these city kids, some of whom had never even heard a cricket chirp, would really go for the brightness of the stars, the sound of frogs and hoot owls and katydids.

Wrong. They were terrified half out of their minds. These kids, who were used to shouts and sirens, were petrified by the stillness of night in the mountains. This time not only did Ruby and Kim cling to us like Velcro, but Mary frantically reached for my hand, Josephine attached herself to Gwen's pajamas, and even the indomitable Estelle stayed as close to us as she could get. Only Latisha walked on ahead, but she leaped whenever something rustled or croaked.

The boys weren't quite as obvious in their terrors, but I could tell by their silence that they were awed. One little kid, sitting between Andy's knees, had his head tipped back about as far as it would go, one finger pointing toward the sky, trying to count the stars. But his other hand was wrapped around Andy's thigh in a death grip.

Connie Kendrick was sitting on a log with a blanket around her shoulders, and when everyone was seated, she just started singing very softly, and one by one, those of us who knew the song joined in: "Kum ba yah, my Lord, Kum ba yah . . ."

When the song was over, Jack Harrigan—as tall as Connie was short—told an Indian legend about the Big Dipper, but I noticed that nobody suggested ghost stories around the fire.

Then a little boy's plaintive cry broke the spell: "I wanna go home," followed by a sob.

Now, a sob around a campfire on the first night away from home, we discovered, is like smallpox in a crowded tent. The cry was immediately followed by a whimper somewhere else, and then I heard Kim give a tearful gulp.

But Connie was ready. "Okay, campers," she called in a loud voice. "What's the Overlook cheer?" And everybody began to yell:

"Clap your hands,
Stamp your feet,
Our Camp Overlook,
Can't be beat!"

"What?" said Connie. "I can hardly hear you. Is that the best you can do?"

**"Clap your hands,
Stamp your feet,
Our Camp Overlook,
Can't be beat!"**

we all shouted, the children loudest of all, as much to drive the homesickness away as to frighten any creatures that might be lurking around.

We sang funny songs next—"Do Your Ears Hang Low"—and then Jack did an imitation of a clown who keeps trying to open an umbrella and hold his pants up at the same time. The kids shrieked out their laughter. Even Kim was giggling in my lap. She was fingering a lock of my hair, twisting it around and around, and I could feel her body shake when she laughed.

I noticed Richard Harrigan smiling at me across the campfire, and suddenly I felt very self-conscious. My hair was wet, my pajamas wrinkled, my Reeboks untied, and a new guy was smiling at me in a warm sort of way. I smiled back. Then I realized he was smiling at all of us, not me alone. Maybe he was feeling the same way I was, that it was just nice to be with friends. Or maybe I was fooling myself and missing Patrick more than I liked to admit. The cool star-filled night—I could almost feel Patrick's arm around me, the way I'd snuggle up against his shoulder. I found myself still missing him at odd moments, wondering where he was and what he was doing. But then it passed, and here I was, cozy in my pajamas and jacket, sharing a campfire in a new place with new people.

Jack went over the schedule for the following day. Then Connie sang a lullaby that she said

Native American mothers sometimes sang to their children, and she told us to go softly back to our cabins and that a bell the next morning would announce breakfast.

Quietly we retraced our steps and, after one more trip to the toilets, crawled into bed by the light from our flashlights. We didn't want to turn on the overhead light because it would break the mood.

We had no sooner got everyone in her bunk than Josephine said she had to go to the bathroom again. I put on my shoes and we went to the toilets.

Ten minutes after I got her in bed the second time, she said she had to go again. I figured this was a bid for attention. "I guess the next time you have to go the bathroom, Josephine, Mary will have to take you," I said.

"Josephine, shut up and go to sleep," came Mary's voice in the darkness.

After that the cabin grew quiet.

Tired as I was, I couldn't fall asleep right away. There were too many things to think about: Dad and Sylvia back home; Estelle's remark in the showers; homesickness for Lester, for the gang; my self-doubt about how good an assistant counselor I would be; Elizabeth and Pamela both liking the same guy; not being in the same cabin with either of them; Richard's smile. . . .

I decided that what I really wanted to happen at camp—in the romance department—was nothing. I wanted a time-out from wondering what guys were thinking about me, from fussing with my hair, using mouthwash in case a guy was going to kiss me. I would like one summer of just being friends with people. Smiling at guys and feeling a certain electric charge, but no blinking lights, no bells, no whistles. . . . Just liking each other without having to get involved. That would be nice.

"Hey, girlfriend," Gwen whispered, sneaking over to my bunk. "You awake?"

"Yeah."

"Me too. You think we're going to make it?"

"I don't know." I scooted over to make room for her, and she sat down on the edge. "Think what the full counselors go through. They've each got seven kids to handle all by themselves. It's all we can do to keep six kids in line between the two of us."

"You know who I miss?" said Gwen.

"Legs?"

"No. Granny."

"Your grandmother?"

"Yeah. She's always lived with us. As long as I can remember, I went in and kissed her before I went to bed. If I was going out for the evening, I'd kiss her before I went out. Isn't that weird? Fifteen years old and still missing my granny?"

"You want my blankie?" I asked, and we giggled. Then I asked, "Really, though, you're not thinking about Legs at all?"

"Not much," she said. "I finally realized he's not right for me, and there's a big wide world out there. . . ."

"Of guys," I added.

"Guys and everything else. Jobs! College! You know what I think? I think Legs was my 'blankie.' The *Boyfriend*, you know? Just to say I had one?"

"He really liked you, though, Gwen."

"Maybe. But we're so different. Isn't it strange how you can go with someone who hardly shares any of your interests and convince yourself he's The One?"

"Love's strange."

"It wasn't love."

"Well, relationships are strange, then," I said. "That's why I want to be totally free for now. The No-Boyfriend Summer."

We sat for a few minutes listening to the crickets through the screen.

"Well, if you want my permission to go call your granny, you've got it," I said finally.

Gwen laughed softly and stood up. "No, I just

needed a heart-to-heart talk with my counselor. G'night, girl. Sleep tight."

I heard the springs squeak as she got into her bunk. And then a voice from somewhere above said, "I could hear everything you said!" and I knew that Estelle had been listening the whole time.

"Watch it, girl-baby," Gwen said.

# 4

# Wet

The next morning I couldn't believe it was time to get up already. I wanted to sleep twice as long and could tell that Gwen felt the same way. Even the girls were awake before us. I had no idea that working with kids could be so exhausting. It wasn't just that hiking was followed by rowing, and volleyball was followed by swimming; about thirty times a day we found ourselves mentally counting heads to be sure nobody had wandered off or drowned or fallen off Point Overlook.

"I've never been so tired in my life," Elizabeth said to us the third evening. "I'm even more tired than when I baby-sit Nathan all day."

"It's the responsibility," said Gwen. "And the fact that we have to stay one step ahead of the girls all the time."

"We've got a girl who cries for her foster mother and keeps begging to call home," said Elizabeth.

"I've got a girl who wets the bed when she gets upset," said Doris Bolden.

A bunch of us were sitting around Pamela and Doris's cabin, putting Band-Aids on our feet and witch hazel on our mosquito bites. If Gwen was the color of cocoa, Doris was the color of nutmeg, and I realized that my mind was once again focused on food. I'd eaten more the first day I'd been there than I eat in two days at home, but I needed every ounce of energy I could get.

The kids were up in the dining hall watching a movie, and the full counselors were supervising so we could have some time off. We'd talked about going swimming in the river, but nobody was making a move in that direction.

Pamela came in from the toilets just then. "Hey!" she said. "I just found out that the guys are skinny-dipping and left their clothes on the bank."

You never saw six girls come alive as fast as we did. Suddenly we weren't as tired as we'd thought. We piled out of the cabin and headed, giggling, toward the river.

There were twelve assistant counselors at camp, six for girls, six for boys. Gwen and Pamela and Elizabeth and I, plus Tommie Lohman and Doris Bolden, made up the assistant counselors in the girls' cabins. Andy Simms, Craig Kimball, Ross Mueller, and Richard Harrigan were assistant counselors on the boys' side, plus a guy we called G. E. and the guy Gwen had her eye on, Joe Ortega.

We went down the path single file. The moon was half full, and the sky was cloudless. We could hear muffled laughter and talk from the guys as they splashed about in the water, and when we came through the trees, we could see their clothes in little heaps there on the ground.

Elizabeth grinned as she went over and sat on top of somebody's jeans and T-shirt. Then the rest of us chose our own little pile, where we sat cross-legged, like pieces on a chessboard, and it wasn't more than a few seconds before the guys saw us.

"Hey, c'mon in! Water's fine!" Ross called.

"No, thanks! We're just looking," Pamela called back, and we laughed.

"Just browsing," called Doris.

"The view from here is great," I told the guys.

They laughed and splashed some more, not rising above waist level, I noticed.

"Oh, this is heaven!" said Gwen. "I think I'll just sit here the rest of the evening."

"Yeah, it's so nice of you guys to leave your clothes for us to sit on," said Tommie. One of the boys splashed water on her, and she just laughed but wouldn't get up.

The guys did all sorts of stunts, like swimming

along underwater, then popping up farther on. We felt so powerful sitting on their clothes, in complete control, none of us willing to leave so they could come out. The movie, we knew, was an hour and a half long. There would be snacks after that, so we had maybe forty minutes left.

"Hey!" Richard Harrigan called finally. "Somebody toss me my pants? Somebody with a good aim, please?"

"Which ones are yours?" called Pamela.

He pointed to the pile that Gwen was sitting on.

"Sorry," Gwen called. "You'll have to come get them."

Now we really hooted. Because Richard was the assistant director's son, we knew that alone would keep him from squealing on us. It's the same with a teacher's or preacher's kid, I think. He goes out of his way to prove he's one of the gang.

The boys laughed too and splashed us some more, but not too much because their clothes, after all, were getting wet. We could tell that there was a lot of whispering going on out there in the water. We couldn't see their faces, but the way they clumped together told us we had them stumped.

"They must be getting cold," Elizabeth said. "The river's cold even in the daytime." She grinned.

"They've been in for at least twenty minutes,"

said Doris. "I don't think I could stand it for more than ten. Not at night."

"Hey, c'mon, girls. You can keep our boxers if you really want them, but could we just have our jeans?" called Andy.

"How are you going to put them on in the water?" I asked.

"There's a bank over there. We'll swim to the other side so as not to offend your delicate sensibilities," said Craig.

We held a conference. They held a conference.

"Nope!" I said. "We like it here just fine. Most comfortable we've been all day."

We figured they'd swim downriver a ways, climb out in the dark, and go back to their cabins to put on something else. We began debating as to what we'd do with their clothes. String their underwear up the flagpole, maybe? Or decorate the trees and bushes with their clothes and be back in the dining hall before they could catch us?

But suddenly there was a great splashing of water, and here the guys came, charging up the riverbank, all six of them buck naked.

We gave a little scream and grabbed on to the guys' clothes so they'd have to wrestle us to get them back, but they didn't even bother with their clothes. I don't know who picked me up—Joe, I think—but each boy grabbed a girl and either dragged or carried her to the water and threw her in.

We gasped and gagged, shocked at this sudden reversal of fortune. And then the boys were in the water with us. We were all laughing and splashing each other with the palms of our hands.

"Hey, girls, you'd swim a lot easier if you didn't have anything on," Ross called.

Pamela giggled. So did Gwen and Tommie.

"Yeah, if anybody wants her shorts unzipped, I'm the man," said Craig, and we laughed some more.

But none of us girls took him up on his offer. We just floated around, watching each other in the moonlight, knowing the boys were totally naked under the water, and now and then colliding with a hairy leg. If Aunt Sally knew what her "little Alice" was doing right now, she'd probably pass out. It was exciting as anything, and Elizabeth looked positively in shock. Delightedly so.

"Hey, next time we go swimming, let's make it coed," said Andy. "Next time you girls have to take it all off."

"Ha! What next time?" said Doris.

"Next movie night. Deal?" said Ross.

"Deal!" said Pamela.

"Pamela!" Elizabeth and I said together, but we laughed, too.

We talked about ourselves then, just the

basics—where we were from, what year we were in school. Craig and Richard, at seventeen, were the only ones who had been assistant counselors at Camp Overlook before.

"What's the hardest part of camp for you?" I asked Andy.

"Trying to keep my boys from sneaking over to peek in the girls' showers," he said, and the others grinned.

"Trying to keep *himself* from sneaking a peek, you mean," said Craig.

"Then my girls are right to worry," I told him. "It's the main topic of conversation in the showers."

Richard told us that the full counselors got Saturday nights off, and the assistant counselors got Friday nights. He said we had from six to midnight to go into town if we wanted, as long as we had one of the older counselors drive.

"Think we could get the camp minibus for the evening?" Craig asked.

"I don't know. Dad might let us. I'll see what I can do," Richard promised, and that was something to look forward to.

We could just make out the dining hall from where we were floating about in the water, and when the lights came on, we knew the movie was over and the kids would be having their snack. We needed to be back there in ten minutes.

So we girls pulled ourselves out of the water, our clothes heavy and clinging, our sneakers squishing with every step we took. We stood on the bank a minute, squeezing water from our shorts, then told the guys good night and hurried back to our cabins to change.

"That was fun!" Elizabeth said breathlessly. "You didn't know where the guys were going to be in the water, and I'm pretty sure my foot touched somebody's . . . well . . . *you* know!"

"No, I *don't* know," Pamela said mischievously. "His what? His ear? His arm?"

But Elizabeth only said, "*You* know" again, and we smiled.

I was thinking back to the time when Elizabeth confessed to me that she had never seen a man naked. I guess her dad never walks between the bedroom and bathroom in his birthday suit, and she hadn't had a little brother yet. So, to help out, I'd gone through a pile of old *National Geographic* magazines looking for naked men, but there always seemed to be a spear or a shield in front of the very places Elizabeth would want to see most.

I had hardly got into a pair of dry shorts when the Coyotes trooped in, looking for us. Mary and Josephine were in the lead, Mary holding Josephine's hand, and were followed by Latisha, looking as belligerent as ever, then Estelle and Ruby and Kim. Kim was near tears because we hadn't been there in the dining hall to escort them back to the cabin and they'd had to set out on their own. Kim clung to Gwen when she came in.

"Where *was* you?" Latisha demanded. "You're our counselors, and I'll bet you been swimming!"

"Right!" I said. "As a matter of fact, I got thrown into the water, and I'm just now drying off."

That shut them up in a hurry. They looked at us wide-eyed.

"Who threw you in?" asked Mary.

"Some of the guys," I told her.

"You gonna tell?" asked Ruby.

"No." Gwen laughed. "It was all in fun."

Kim still seemed on the verge of tears. "I don't want anybody to throw me in," she said.

"I won't let anyone do that to you, girl-baby," Gwen purred. "And if somebody did, I'd be right there to pull you out, so don't you worry." She put both arms around Kim and held her close, and that just seemed to be the opening bell, because all the other girls edged in for a hug. Even Estelle. But Latisha watched with a jaundiced eye.

"Bet one of 'em's your boyfriend," Latisha said to Gwen.

"Yeah? Which one?" Gwen said.

"I don't know. Andy somebody?"

"Nice guy," said Gwen. "But what about Joe?"

"Ohhhh! Jooooe!" the girls chorused.

Latisha gave a hoot. "They're gonna go off behind the cabins and kiiisss!" she said.

Gwen just smiled at her and looked mysterious, but the girls were still giggling and grinning.

"Well, *are* you?" Estelle asked.

And when Gwen raised an eyebrow, Estelle said, in a hoity-toity voice, "Are you going to go behind the cabins and *make love*?"

Now the girls really hooted.

"Joe is just a friend of mine, like all the other guys here are friends. We just met," said Gwen.

"She going to!" Latisha stage-whispered, and the girls went laughing and giggling to the showers.

There was an incident Wednesday night that almost got Pamela's cabin mate, Doris Bolden, dismissed from camp.

She and Pamela had a particularly difficult girl in their cabin, a nine-year-old named Virginia, who was living in her third foster home, and had a vocabulary that would have shocked a sailor. When somebody displeased her, her first reaction was to clobber them on the head or the back, or make a quick jab with her elbow.

Doris had warned her that there would be

consequences if she physically attacked another child again, but that night in the showers she knocked a girl down for using her towel, and when Doris grabbed her, she'd yelled, "Get your hands off me, nigger."

Pamela and Doris's girls had come down early and showered with us, as the girls in cabins eight and ten had cleanup duty in the dining hall that evening. So Gwen and I saw the whole thing. Punishment had to be swift and sure.

"Get dressed, Virginia," Doris had said. "You and I are going for a walk."

Gwen and I didn't think much about it. I thought that Pamela would probably get the other girls to bed, and then Doris would take Virginia for a "cool down" and discuss what had happened in the showers.

Back in our own cabin we went through the nightly ritual of confiscating the food that Ruby and Mary—the usual culprits—had sneaked out of the dining hall in fists or pockets, promising that if they got hungry, the food would be right there in our metal lockbox waiting for them. They didn't have to steal, only ask.

Mary insisted that Josephine say her prayers at night, and Ruby and Estelle said theirs as well. I asked the other girls to keep a respectful silence while they prayed.

Then we had a few stories while lying in our beds with the light off—made-up stories and tales about what had gone on during the day—when suddenly there came the most terrible far-off scream . . . then another and another, followed by loud sobbing.

I think the entire camp was on alert. If we heard a disturbance, our first duty, we'd been told, was to check for fire, and if there was no fire, we were to keep the girls in our cabins until there was word over the sound system as to what we should do in an emergency.

Gwen and I were on our feet instantly, staring through the screen door, but there was no smell of smoke or hint of fire. There was, however, the sound of running feet and a flashlight coming from the direction of the camp director's cabin, another coming from Jack Harrigan's.

The screams came again, then we heard Doris Bolden saying, "Hey, be quiet now," and finally, as we all gawked, our girls gathering behind us at the cabin door and windows, we saw Doris and Virginia and Connie and Jack all coming back from the campfire circle, Virginia crying loudly. They dropped Virginia off at Pamela's cabin, but Doris was escorted to the camp office.

When we'd got our girls settled down again at last, Gwen and I whispered together outside our cabin, trying to figure out what could have happened.

"You don't think Doris would hit her, do you?" Gwen whispered.

I shook my head.

Obviously, however, something terrifying had happened. It wasn't until the next day that we found out. Pamela told us.

As punishment for pushing a girl down in the shower, Doris had taken Virginia out to the campfire circle. She'd told Virginia that she was to sit alone on a log and think about how she could control her temper in the future and that Doris would be back for her later.

Doris had not actually left. She had gone back in the trees to keep watch over her, but Virginia had panicked, terrified at being alone at night. She would have preferred "getting smacked," she'd told Connie between sobs.

In Connie's office Doris had been lectured and almost let go. The whole idea of camp, Connie had said, was to get city kids in tune with nature, not to scare them with it, and with that punishment, she had set Virginia back even further than she'd been when she came.

But because Doris was well liked by the other little girls and had not actually left the child alone, it was decided that she would stay here on probation and apologize to Virginia, which she did. She had gone back to their cabin, Pamela reported, where Virginia was still sniffling and, in front of the other girls, had told Virginia that she had made a serious mistake in making her think she was alone out there in the dark, that she would never have left her alone unwatched.

Doris assured her that it would not happen again but that if Virginia continued to hit other girls, she would have to sit in the director's office for a long time-out and would miss the next movie as well.

That seemed a fair punishment all around. Doris kept her job and her dignity, Virginia received the apology and the warning she deserved, and the rest of the assistant counselors got a lesson in discipline.

"It's like walking a tightrope," Tommie said. "One step to the left, you've gone too far. One step to the right, you haven't been assertive enough."

"It'll take every single bit of patience I've got," said Gwen.

"And you'd better not have your mind on anything else, because you need to concentrate totally on your girls," said Pamela. She sighed. "Maybe that's a good thing. It'll keep me from worrying about Mom and what *she's* up to."

Nobody spoke for a moment. Then I asked, "So

what's going to keep us going for the next two weeks?"

This time Elizabeth and Pamela both grinned. "Friday night," said Pamela. "Assistant counselors' night out!"

# 5

# Gerald

Gwen and I tried not to have favorites among the Coyotes because they were each needy in a different way. Kim needed all the reassurance she could get, and Ruby seemed to sail through the week without any particular problems as long as she got hugs now and then. But Latisha was mad at the world and took it out verbally on anyone who was handy.

"What you looking at, girl?" had been her first comment to Estelle the day we arrived, and of course Estelle had issues before Latisha even opened her mouth.

"Not you, that's for sure," Estelle had said, and the way Latisha bristled, we were prepared for flare-ups between the two.

But Mary and Josephine were my own little case study, as Gwen put it. I couldn't figure out why Mary felt so responsible for her sister—doing things for her that Josephine could probably do herself. At our first staff session I talked to Connie Kendrick about putting one of the sisters in another cabin.

"Better not," Connie said. "We had to pull a lot of strings to get them here in the first place, and they finally came on the condition that they not be separated. We take what we can get, and these two kids really needed a break from home." She winked at me. "Of course, they don't have to stick together like Siamese twins. There's no reason you can't be creative."

So at breakfast on Thursday, as Mary led Josephine to our table, I said, "I can't decide which of you two girls I want to sit beside most. So I'm just going to have to sit between you, and then I'll have one of you on each side. Lucky me!"

Mary paused a moment, then smiled and, letting go of her sister's hand, allowed me to slide between them on the bench.

"Mission accomplished," murmured Gwen, and I caught her smile from across the table.

Later that morning, as Jack Harrigan led the kids on a nature hike and the assistant counselors tagged along, G. E. came up beside me. His real name, he'd told us, was Gerald Eggers, but his friends all called him G. E. And I wondered sympathetically if that was because he was shaped like a hanging lightbulb, smaller at the top than the bottom—narrow chest and shoulders, heavy legs. He had a terrific voice, though. If you closed your eyes and listened to him, it was only his voice that was important.

"So how's it going?" he asked. "This your first time being a counselor?"

"Assistant counselor," I answered, and nodded. "You almost need a degree in psychology to know what's going on with these kids."

He chuckled. "First time for me too. But you seem a natural with the kids. Thinking about teaching somewhere down the line?"

"No. Psychology, actually."

"Yeah? I'd like to work with children. I was thinking about pediatrics, but I doubt I could get into med school. So I suppose I'll go into teaching."

Elizabeth and Pamela moved up behind us then, and G. E. went on ahead to walk with Ross and Craig.

"Guess who Gwen's pairing off with," Pamela said. "Joe."

"What do you mean, pairing off?" I asked.

"He had his arm around her back there."

I gave a quick glance behind me. Joe Ortega was giving Gwen a shoulder massage. "Good for Gwen," I said, grinning.

"Where do you suppose we'll go tomorrow night? What's in town?" asked Elizabeth.

"Richard says there's a place that has line dancing and a lot of the counselors hang out there on their night off," Pamela told us.

"I'm ready for a break," said Elizabeth.

"A Ross break," said Pamela.

"I saw him first," said Elizabeth.

"No, you didn't," said Pamela. "He's mine!"

There was an hour of music after the hike. Whenever there's a special program, the assistant counselors get some time off, seeing as how we don't get paid. It's a chance to wash our underwear or call home or just nap. But I decided to go for a walk by myself. I wanted to take in the scents and sounds of the woods without a bunch of chattering kids around me, so I set out for the overlook.

I was halfway down the path when I heard someone say, "Mind if I join you?"

I turned to see Gerald walking briskly up behind me.

I really didn't want him along. I didn't want anyone along, actually.

"Or did you want to be alone?" he asked, looking at me uncertainly.

I didn't have the heart to tell him to go back.

"Oh, I was just trying to get away from the noise of camp—give my ears a rest," I said.

"I know what you mean." And then, unsure of himself, he said, "But if you'd rather I didn't come . . ."

*Oh, for Pete's sake, don't be so wishy-washy!* I thought. "Of course not," I said, and walked on. He gave a little skip to catch up.

Isn't it strange how just the slightest mannerism can turn you off? That little skip, and I knew for certain I could not feel romantic about Gerald Eggers in a million years.

"Penny for your thoughts," said Gerald.

I sighed and closed my eyes. He wasn't just in my face, he was in my head.

"Thinking about this summer, that's all. This'll be the longest I've ever been away from home," I said.

"Homesick?"

"Not really. I'm just hoping I can hold out another two weeks. Kids can sure be exhausting. I can't imagine what it's like to be a mother and be around little children all day."

"I think you'd make a great mother," said Gerald.

"That's a long way off," I said. I was beginning to get bad vibes.

"I had a cousin who married at eighteen, and

she's really happy," said Gerald. "She's a great mother, too."

"Good for her," I said.

"I guess that's the first thing I look for in a girl," Gerald went on. "How she gets along with kids tells me what kind of mother she'd make."

I stared straight ahead. Was this a test? *Oh, brother.* Was this guy looking for wife material at the grand age of fifteen? If I said I loved children, would he propose? Ask me to wait for him while he worked his way through grad school?

I found myself suddenly babbling on about school and how I'd be entering tenth grade in the fall and how long I'd been on the newspaper staff and what had happened during our production of *Fiddler on the Roof* and how my dad was marrying my seventh-grade English teacher—anything to change the subject—and then I realized it might sound as though I were trying to impress him, show him I was the kind of girl he wanted to marry. My jaw snapped shut.

He glanced over at me. "Get a bug in your mouth?" he asked.

"No, my foot," I said. He gave me a quizzical smile.

We'd reached the end of the path and were facing the low stone wall, the overlook beyond. It was a gorgeous day, and the taller trees were spreading their shadows out over the ones below. All the assorted greens of summer were stretching before us, and beyond the trees the blue and purple layers of hills grew fainter and fainter in the distance. If I couldn't be alone, why couldn't Richard have followed me up here, or Andy or Craig?

And then I felt an arm around my waist as Gerald edged in closer to my side. Yikes! He *was* going to propose! He'd get down on one knee and pull a gold-plated ring out of his pocket—one size fits all—and . . . I moved away and went over to lean my elbows on the stone wall.

"Sorry," said G. E. "I guess I moved a little too fast."

The third reason not to like him. I swallowed. "I'm really not looking for romance this summer, Gerald," I said.

I heard him sigh. "Let me guess," he said. "You're about to give me that 'I like you as a friend, but . . .' line."

"And?"

"Well, you aren't the first girl who's said it."

"Maybe you come on a little too strong too fast," I said.

"So if I slow down, do I have a chance?"

It just seemed that everything Gerald said made it worse. He seemed so desperate, as though he had to pin down the rest of his life—his love life, anyway—in case he never got another chance.

"Maybe sometimes it's better to make a girl worry a little that you *won't* like her," I said.

He gave a small laugh. "That'll be the day."

I wanted to get back to camp. Even sitting on my bunk flossing my teeth seemed more exciting than continuing this conversation with Gerald. I started back along the path. "Sometimes it's nice just to be friends, G. E. You don't have to make it anything special," I said. "Okay?"

"The story of my life," Gerald said morosely. He put his hands in his pockets, and we walked along in silence for a while.

I thought of a girl I knew back in junior high who didn't have a lot of friends and finally stood in front of a train. It *didn't* exactly help to tell someone just to forget about having somebody special. There wasn't anyone special in *my* life just then, but I felt pretty sure there would be someday. Why was Gerald worrying about that now?

"Well, thanks for being honest with me," he said when we got close to camp again.

And that's where I lost it. "G. E., *listen* to yourself! We've not even been here a week, I hardly know you, and you tell me you're looking for a girl who's good with children. I'm not thinking that far ahead! I've got a lot of living to do, and so do you. Be a radio announcer or something. Be a singer!"

"I am a singer," said Gerald. "How did you know?"

I was so relieved to have something else to talk about that I actually smiled. "Because you've got a great voice. You've got the best-sounding voice of any guy here. I'll bet you sing bass."

He grinned a little. "I do. I sing with the madrigals at our school."

"See?" I said. "You just need to get reacquainted with your good points. G. E., meet Gerald. Gerald . . . G. E." He laughed, and so, finally, did I.

When I got back to our cabin, I faced a drama of a different sort. The Coyotes were back from the music program, and Gwen was having a face-off with Estelle. Gwen's voice was loud: "I don't care what you thought Latisha was saying about you, girl! If you've got any complaints, you bring them to me. You don't go dumping someone else's stuff on the floor."

"She got my shoes!" Latisha was shouting. "She done something with my shoes!"

"Have you got Latisha's shoes, Estelle?" Gwen demanded.

Estelle was just begging for a fight, I could tell. Tossing her long black hair behind her, she thrust her face forward, scrunched up her eyes and nose, and said, in a mocking voice, "No, I don't have her stinking shoes, smelling up the place." And then she muttered, "Those nigger-smelling feet."

It took both Gwen and me to pull Latisha off her and get the girls separated.

"She think niggers smell, she ought to smell her own shit," shouted Latisha. "Her shit smells worse'n anybody's, all that dog food she eats."

Now it was Estelle lunging for Latisha. This time I took hold of her and kept her back. Kim was cowering on her bunk, about as far away as she could get, and Mary had Josephine on her lap and was rocking her back and forth. Ruby simply watched from a top bunk, swinging her legs.

*Don't get stuck on the language here,* I told myself, remembering the advice in our handbook. *Focus on the feelings behind the words.* Estelle had prejudice, Latisha had attitude, and Latisha most of all wanted her shoes back.

I gripped Estelle by the shoulders and looked her square in the eyes. "Where are Latisha's shoes?"

Estelle tossed her head again. "Out there."

"Out where?"

She pointed and I went to the door to look. Latisha's sneakers, the laces tied together, had been tossed up over a sign strung above the road outside the cabins. An arrow pointed up the hill toward the dining hall. Latisha's sneakers hung down over the "c" in "Office."

Gwen and I looked at each other. "Why did you do that?" she asked Estelle.

"I *told* you why!" Estelle countered. "Latisha's always leaving them for me to stumble over, and they stink!"

"No worse'n yours do!" Latisha shouted.

"And Latisha's always bossing us around, telling people what to do," said Estelle.

"Yeah? She bossier than *me*. She thinks *she's* white too!" said Latisha. "*She's* colored too, ain't she, Alice? You got taco blood in you, you're colored."

"Okay, here's the deal," said Gwen. "We've got two girls who have to learn to get along with each other and a pair of sneakers dangling over the wire out there. You've got till three o'clock this afternoon to figure out a way to get them down, and you have to do it together. You can't ask anyone else to do it for you. If you're still enemies but you get them down, you get one point. If you get them down and you're not enemies anymore, you get two points. And if you get them down and decide to be *friends* the rest of the time we're here, you get three points."

"So what do we get with the points?" asked Latisha.

"One point, you get an extra bag of popcorn at the movie Saturday night. Two points, you get two bags of popcorn and a Milky Way. Three points . . ."

"Three points you have to kiss Joe Ortega in front of us!" said Estelle.

The cabin suddenly erupted in laughter, Latisha and Estelle both hooting together.

"You got it!" said Gwen, looking a little unnerved. "You get the shoes down and figure out how to be friends, and Joe and I will kiss right here in the doorway for all to see."

The Coyotes squealed and carried on, hands over their mouths, eyes wide with delight. We herded them to the dining hall for lunch.

Afterward it took some doing, but Estelle and Latisha finally borrowed a stepladder from the caretaker, carried it down to the cabin, and set it up, under Gwen's supervision. Estelle got an oar from the boathouse, climbed halfway up, with Latisha holding the ladder steady, and managed to knock the sneakers off the sign. They fell to the ground with a thud.

Estelle looked at Latisha uncertainly, but there was devilment in her eyes. "Okay, we're friends," she said.

"Really?" I asked.

Latisha gave a shrug. "Yeah," she said.

"Is this a promise that you'll really try?" asked Gwen.

Now Latisha was grinning. "Yeah. Now you got to go get Joe."

After Estelle climbed down and the ladder was returned, Gwen went in search of Joe Ortega and brought him grinning to the door of the cabin, the boys from his own cabin trailing curiously behind.

"Okay, girls, get ready," Joe said. He glanced up toward the office. "Nobody looking, are they? You want to see me kiss this lady?"

"Yessssss!" all the girls chorused, and kids from other cabins gathered too.

Joe Ortega put one arm around Gwen's waist, the other under her shoulders, and dramatically swooped her backward, giving her a movie-star kiss. All the little campers clapped and screeched hysterically.

And suddenly I looked up to see Legs coming down the hill from the parking lot.

# 6

# A Little Lesson in Growing Up

It was like a movie. One minute we were watching Gwen and Joe in their movie-star embrace, accompanied by all the squealing kids, and the next we were watching long-legged Leo coming down the hill toward us, taking in the whole scene.

"Uh . . . Gwen," I said. "Company."

Joe brought her back to a standing position, then said to the little group from his own cabin, "And *that's* the way you kiss a lady." Then he saw Legs right in front of him, and I heard Gwen gasp.

I guess the next scene in a movie would be Legs punching Joe in the mouth, but that didn't happen. Legs looked at Joe a moment, then at Gwen, and said, "Well, hello."

"You drove all the way up here?" Gwen asked. We could see Jack Harrigan coming down the hill from the office.

"I didn't fly," Legs said in answer. "Just wanted

to see how you're doing. Looks to me like you're having a pretty good time."

"Legs, this is Joe, my friend here at camp. Joe, this is Leo, from school," said Gwen.

Jack came up to us then. "Hello?" he said to Legs, a question mark in his voice. He put out his hand and Legs shook it.

"Leo Green," Legs said. "I'm a friend of Gwen's."

"We're glad to have you drop in, but all visitors have to register first at the office," Jack said cordially. "Our counselors are on twenty-four-hour duty here, so . . . I hope you understand. We generally limit visitors to Sundays."

In the movies Legs probably would have turned and pasted the assistant director in the mouth too, but that didn't happen either.

"Well, I work Sundays, and this is the only time I could get off. I just want to talk with Gwen for a few minutes," Legs said.

"Sure. You want to come up to the dining hall?" Jack waited. I'll bet he could smell trouble at fifty paces.

"I'll be right back," Gwen said to the rest of us, and, turning to Estelle and Latisha, she said, "Okay, girls. You did good! Now keep it up, hear?"

The kids only gawked.

Legs and Gwen went up toward the dining hall,

Jack walking about ten feet behind them. Joe nodded in their direction and looked at me. "Is Leo bad news?" he asked.

"I don't know," I said honestly. It was really Gwen's story to tell, not mine.

It was time for the canoe lesson, so we guided the campers down to the river.

Connie was on the bank giving instructions through a bullhorn, starting with the safety talk about the right way to get in and out of a canoe while Tommie gave a demonstration. Then Ross took a canoe out into the water to show the kids the correct way to hold a paddle and a few of the basic strokes.

"Everyone will have a chance to go out in a canoe," Connie said. "Some of you will get to paddle, and some of you will just go along for the ride. But before camp is over, we want everyone who would like to learn to paddle to have a chance."

We lined the kids up in pairs, an older and a younger camper, and put life jackets on them. They reminded me of Chinese wontons, their heads the lumps in the middle, and they laughed and hooted at the sight of themselves.

It was when we actually tried to get them in the canoes that the trouble started. Kim was terrified, and one of Elizabeth's charges clung to her and wouldn't let go. Mary, of course, insisted that Josephine go in the same canoe with her.

Each fearful camper got the personal attention of a counselor, and I had to admire the way G. E. calmed Kim. He simply took her by both hands till she stopped trembling, and then, each taking a step sideways, G. E. counting all the while, "*one* banana, *two* banana . . . ," they moved together toward the water and he got her to sit in the middle of a canoe.

We held the canoes steady while the kids got in. After each of the dozen or so canoes received its passengers, the counselor in the stern moved it out into the water. The rest of the campers waited their turn on the bank.

As each counselor gave directions to the older camper in the bow of their canoe, the campers awkwardly brandished their paddles, while the younger passenger in the middle either dangled his or her arms over the sides, prepared to enjoy the adventure, or sat frozen, as though the very act of breathing might overturn them all. But after about ten minutes of slowly moving out over the water, even the fearful ones, Kim included, looked as though they could enjoy it.

Once the kids got the hang of it, Connie called out instructions for the C stroke and the J stroke, so that they were turning this way and that, and

Jack Harrigan came back from the dining hall to patrol the perimeter in his own canoe.

From where I stood on the bank with the campers still waiting their turn, I saw Gwen coming down the hill. Elizabeth looked over too, searching her face, and then Gwen gave us the okay sign. Not only that, but she was smiling. From somewhere back by the parking lot, we could hear the sound of a car pulling out and heading off down the mountain road. Gwen silently lifted a fist in the air and mouthed, *Yes!* When we saw Joe looking at her, we all laughed.

I couldn't say that the canoe lesson went especially well, but for kids who had never been on a river before, I think they did a pretty fair job. The canoes were going in circles, some more jerkily than others, but the counselors kept them far enough apart that they didn't bump into each other, and every child who wanted to try—and even some who didn't—had a chance to sit in front and paddle. In fact, I didn't do so bad either. Andy let me sit in the bow of his canoe, and though I managed to drop my paddle in the water and we had to chase it down—the kids jeering— it felt good to learn something I'd never done before.

"At the end of our third week, campers, we're going to have a canoe race, and we'll see which of our cabins wins," Connie told them. And the air was filled with shouts of "We will!" "No, we're gonna win!"

At one point, when the kids took a lemonade break, Pamela, Elizabeth, and I crowded around Gwen.

"What happened?" I asked.

"Legs came all the way up here to tell me that our trip to Baltimore is off when I get back, because his grandma is sick, and he's going to be spending all that time in Baltimore with her," Gwen said, grinning. "I just happen to know that the girl I've heard he's seeing on the side told her friends that she's going to Baltimore that exact same week. Not only that, but Legs's grandma lives in Frederick. I told him that if there was one thing I couldn't stand it was a cheatin' man and that he was crossed off my list as of yesterday. You should have seen the relief on his face!" She laughed some more.

It was a good day at Camp Overlook.

Except that when the canoes went out and came in a second time with another batch of kids, Mary didn't wait for us to help her out. My back was turned momentarily as I helped Estelle make the jump to the bank. When I turned around, Mary and Josephine were starting to climb out of their canoe by themselves. Josephine stumbled climbing over the side, and because the girls were holding hands, both went into the water.

Camp Overlook's philosophy is to let campers experience the consequences of their actions unless it's a question of safety, and neither girl, of course, went under. They bobbed about on the surface in their life jackets, and the surprise in Josephine's tiny face soon gave way to delight when she discovered she could not sink if she tried. In fact, she could maneuver any way she wanted.

It was Mary who went bananas, even though the water wasn't over their heads.

"Josie!" she screamed. "Josie, grab my hand! Paddle over here!"

But the more she yelled, the more Josephine grinned and dog-paddled away. Gwen and I were both ready to jump in after them—Ross was already in the water—but we caught Jack Harrigan shaking his head. He motioned for Ross to just circle the girls and let them get the feel of moving about in the water and staying afloat.

"Alice!" Mary screamed. "Gwen! You come get us!"

"Your sister seems to be doing okay, Mary," Jack called. "Can you see why we wanted you to get out of the canoe one at a time?"

"She's going to drown!" she kept bawling, horrified to see Josephine moving farther and farther away from her in the water, with no one going after her. It was painful to listen to the terror in her voice.

Ross corralled Josephine at last and brought her in, and we got the girls back to our cabin and into dry clothes, Gwen set about combing Josephine's matted hair and I motioned Mary to join me for a private walk. I wasn't sure what I was going to say, but all the assistant counselors were told to squeeze in as many one-on-one walks as we could, and the kids adored it. It was a sign that the chosen boy or girl was special.

I held Mary's hand.

"I guess that was pretty scary," I said.

"I almost drowned! So did Josephine, and you would've let her!" she declared.

I gave her hand a playful tug. "Do you really believe that, Mary? You knew we were right there, and Josie showed us she was okay."

Mary just shook her head. "She could've drowned, though. She's not ever going to grow up right."

"Why not?"

"She's too little," Mary said. "She was born too soon. Mama said."

"Really?"

Mary let go of my hand to demonstrate. "Mama

says she was only *this* big!" She held her hands about eight inches apart, then grabbed hold of mine again.

"Boy, that *is* little!" I said. "Look how much she's grown!"

"She's still too little. When she came home from the hospital, we had to watch to see that she didn't stop breathing. Well . . . I don't remember that, but my uncle says so. Everything Josephine does, I have to watch she doesn't hurt herself."

I looked down at the top of Mary's head—only two years older than her sister's—and wondered just what Mary would do with herself if she didn't have Josephine to watch over. I was beginning to get a handle on the problem.

"Well, you sure must have done a good job, Mary, because look at all Josie can do!" I said. "And guess what? When she's a grown girl, she can tell her friends that her big sister showed her how to do everything herself."

Mary continued walking, her round face in a frown. I hoped I knew what I was talking about. "The more you let Josephine do for herself, the more you're teaching her how to grow up."

"She makes a lot of mistakes!" said Mary, rolling her eyes.

"So do I!" I said. "But that's the way I learn. And I'll bet you'll be a very good teacher."

• • •

Friday evening we gathered in Elizabeth and Tommie's cabin to get ready for our big night out. Gwen, sitting on the edge of a bunk, was replaiting one of her cornrows. I noticed her black bra.

"Black! Hmm!" I smiled.

"Hey! You put on a white bra and I don't make any comment," she teased.

"It's not the same and you know it," said Pamela. "Not if it's lace, it's not!"

"She's not going to keep it on long, anyway," Tommie said, and we laughed.

"It's her underpants I'm worried about," I said. I tugged at Gwen's jeans. "Let's see your undies, Gwen. Is there lace on those, too?" She playfully pushed me away.

And then Elizabeth, her face slightly flushed, dropped something on Gwen's lap. "Just in case," she said.

Gwen looked down at the box of Trojans resting on her thighs. "Get *outta* here girl!" she cried, as we all burst into laughter.

"You just might need them," Elizabeth said.

"Get *out*!" Gwen repeated.

Pamela grabbed the Trojans from Gwen and examined the package. "'*Ribbed*'? '*Prelubricated*'? '*For maximum pleasure*'? Aha! What do *you* know about these kinds of things, Liz?"

Elizabeth's face was fiery red in spite of herself. "I . . . I just grabbed the first package I saw," she said. Then, looking around at us, she said, "Why? Didn't I get the right kind?"

Tommie took the box next and examined it. Without cracking a smile, she said, "Are you sure they're the right size?"

Elizabeth's face fell. "There are . . . sizes?"

We all tried to keep a straight face.

"Of course!" said Tommie. "Extra small, small, average, large, extra large, super stud . . ." She tossed the box back to Gwen.

I thought my face was going to explode, I was trying so hard not to laugh.

"But how do you *know*?" Elizabeth asked in bewilderment.

"You have to *measure*, Elizabeth!" said Pamela. "You have to carry several different sizes with you and bring a ruler and—"

Elizabeth suddenly caught on, and when we burst into laughter, she said, "Oh . . . you . . . *guys!*" and laughed a little too.

"Listen," said Doris, "I really want to know. Did you actually buy these yourself?"

"She *did!*" I volunteered.

"Yes, but I couldn't find them at first," Elizabeth continued, "and then a clerk asked if he could help. I was so *embarrassed!*"

"So what did you tell him?" Tommie asked. "That you wanted some ribbed condoms with a lubricated tip?"

"No! I just said I wanted some men's condoms."

"*Men's* condoms?" Pamela shrieked, and we were off again.

Elizabeth sat helplessly down on her bunk bed. "He sent me over to women's sanitary products, and right beside them were all these little boxes with pictures of a man and woman doing romantic stuff."

"So why did you choose this kind?" Gwen asked.

"I liked the sunset," Elizabeth said, and we doubled over. She told the rest of the story then: the lines at the checkout counter, the price check . . .

"Liz, it could only happen to you," said Pamela.

"Yeah, but why are you giving them to me?" Gwen said to Elizabeth. "You think the first time I go out with a guy I'm going to get naked?"

"Don't get mad," said Elizabeth. "I just don't want any of us to get into trouble."

"If you don't want them, Gwen, I'll take them," Pamela offered, plucking the box from Gwen's hand. "If Ross and I hook up . . ."

"I didn't buy them for you and Ross!" said Elizabeth hotly.

"Don't tell me we're going to have a catfight right here," said Tommie. She grabbed the condoms out of Pamela's hand and turned to Doris.

"You take them," she said.

"I'm in enough hot water as it is," Doris said. "I'm lucky I didn't get kicked out of camp. Nope. I don't plan to worry about this stuff till I'm married."

"We could give them to Gerald," said Tommie.

"G. E.?" we all asked in surprise.

"Yeah. He's been following me around all afternoon telling me how he's turned on by girls who get along with kids—how it means they'd make good wives and mothers."

I stared. "That's what he told *me* this morning! The very same thing."

We all looked at each other. "Now there's a guy who wants to fall in love," said Gwen. "So who's going to put him out of his misery?"

"Don't look at me," said Doris.

We all turned toward Elizabeth.

"Let's tell him Elizabeth loves her little brother," Pamela said.

"Yeah, let's say that she *adores* kids and that her greatest wish in life is to be a faithful wife and mother," said Gwen.

"Hey, guys!" said Elizabeth.

"I'll say she lets them snuggle up to her in bed," said Tommie.

"Oh, stop it!" Elizabeth said, swatting at us.

We finished getting ready and probably looked the best we had since we'd come. We'd showered, blow-dried our hair, put on lip gloss and mascara. Two of the paid counselors, Phil and Sue, were going to take us to a restaurant called the White Rooster, and after the mandatory lecture from Jack about none of us going into the bar section, nobody leaving the building and going off alone, we set off in the camp's minibus.

It felt good to get away for the evening. Everything seemed dark and mysterious on the winding dirt road with no lights other than those on the minibus.

Sue had the radio going, and when we weren't chattering away, we were humming along with the music—everyone but me, of course. I won't even hum in public; clearly, I was the only counselor at Camp Overlook who couldn't carry a tune.

Suddenly Elizabeth leaned against my shoulder and whispered, "So who has them, do you know?"

"Has what?" I whispered back.

"The condoms. Nobody gave them back."

"I don't know," I told her. "The last person who had them was Tommie, I think. Or was it Pamela?"

I felt Elizabeth stiffen beside me, but then the lights of the White Rooster came into view, and we soon piled out of the car.

# Night Out

"C'mon," Phil said, and led us over to a table by the dance floor in the restaurant. It was a big high-ceilinged room with bare rafters overhead and old signs decorating the walls—signs advertising Burma-Shave and Ivory Flakes and twenty-five-cent chili dogs. We ordered sodas, and they were brought to our table with a big bowl of peanuts. The band was playing a country song, and couples in western dress were already whirling around out on the floor.

"So how goes it?" Phil asked us over the music. "Think you can stick it out for two more weeks?"

"As long as we get Fridays off," Ross said.

"Can the *kids* hold out? That's the question," said Tommie.

"I think only a couple of kids have been sent home in the past couple of years," said Sue. "Most kids are pretty tough."

"Besides, they'll all want to go on the Kelpie Hunt," said Phil, grinning mysteriously.

"Yeah, what *is* that?" I asked. "I've seen it on the schedule."

"The Kelpie Hunt," Phil said, "is what we do on the last night. It's like a ghost walk. We'll get them psyched up for this two weeks in advance, so they can work up their nerve. Nobody wants to admit he's scared, so they all stick it out."

"What's a kelpie?" I asked.

Richard faked surprise. "You never heard of a kelpie?" I saw him wink at Phil. "Well," he said. "I guess you'll have to stick around and find out."

"Yeah," said Craig. "We'll give the girls a sneak preview."

Sue laughed. "They always do this," she told us. "A camp tradition."

Something else to look forward to. I was really beginning to like Camp Overlook. I liked sitting here at a table with a bunch of new friends—old friends, too.

When the music stopped, we saw people getting into position for line dancing. I'd never done any—I don't know that Elizabeth or Pamela had either—but Elizabeth's taken all kinds of dance lessons, and she can pick up almost any step. So there we were in three rows in the middle of the floor, side-stepping along and tapping our heels on the beat.

To tell the truth, I never did figure out for sure what we were doing. I managed to pick up a simple step, which I repeated over and over as we moved across the floor. But half the fun was coming in a second late on the scuff or the stomp or the hop or the jump and laughing along with the others. When we finished one sequence, I found we'd turned and were facing a different direction.

The seasoned line dancers put up with us good-naturedly, and when one of the fiddle players called out to me that I was doing fine, I knew immediately that I wasn't. But I didn't care, because some of the guys weren't doing so hot either, and we cast each other funny, sympathetic glances. As the music went from "Whatcha Gonna Do with a Cowboy" to "I Feel Lucky," and the dance changed from Cowboy Motion to the Freeze, I discovered that it didn't much matter what I did as long as I could keep from bumping into someone. I was having a great time.

G. E. had positioned himself next to Elizabeth, I noticed, and kept giving her a special smile whenever she looked in his direction. When the music stopped a second time and we took a break, he put one hand on her waist as they left the floor, guiding her back to our table, and I almost laughed out loud.

All us girls trooped to the rest room then, and as

soon as we got inside, Elizabeth said, "Somebody else has to dance next to Gerald next time."

"What'd he do? Paw you?" asked Doris.

"No. He's a clinger. Pamela, you dance next to him. He'll be scared of you."

"Why?"

"Just act normal. Make a pass at him. I'll bet he'll run for his life," Elizabeth said.

"I'll bet he won't."

"Extra-large Coke?" said Tommie. "I'm betting he will too. I'll bet he's the kind of guy who would be scared to death if a girl made the first move."

"Okay. If he doesn't, what do I do?" said Pamela. "Who can I pass him off on?"

"We'll think of something," said Doris.

I began to feel sorry for G. E. Did guys think the same thing about girls who seemed as desperate? I wondered how I'd feel if a guy made a pass at me and I found out later it was on a dare. Still, Gerald *did* act like a dork at times, and if anybody could discourage him, it was Pamela.

We got back to the table and saw that Phil and Sue were holding hands. And for the first time I noticed Sue wearing an engagement ring. They were our most senior counselors, next to Connie and Jack, and I wondered if they'd met here—if love had blossomed at Camp Overlook. I could see how it could happen.

There was definitely something exciting about being away from home overnight, even for me, the Girl Who Wasn't Looking for Romance. Just being up here in the mountains with six available guys around, I guess, gave me the feeling that maybe we'd go a little further than we ordinarily would.

When we got back out on the floor for the second set, Ross was dancing between Pamela and Elizabeth, Gerald on the other side of Pamela. The dancing was even more vigorous this time, and I stumbled over my feet a lot. I felt as though everyone else was wearing tap shoes and I was wearing clogs. But when the number was over, Pamela suddenly threw her arms around Gerald's neck and kissed him, a long hard kiss on the lips, like a dramatic flourish to the end of the dance.

Gerald didn't move away. He held his hands tentatively on Pamela's waist, but he didn't try to prolong the kiss, either. There was an embarrassed, fake smile on his face, and I think we all cringed when we realized that Gerald wasn't enough of a dork not to know that this was a put-up job.

What Pamela didn't see, though, was that when she moved away from Ross on one side of her for that dramatic kiss with Gerald, Ross missed it entirely, because he had turned toward Elizabeth, lifted her hair up off the nape of her neck, and was gently blowing on her to cool her down.

*Hey, hey!* I thought.

Elizabeth looked absolutely radiant.

It was a good night. For everyone but Gerald, I guess. On the way back to camp Richard and Craig taught us a bawdy song the counselors had made up one year, sung to the tune of "Oh, Susannah."

> Oh, she came from south of Overlook,
> A virgin tried and true,
> She'd saved herself for Billy Boy,
> Back in Timbuktu.

> But Billy Boy was feeling sad,
> And found himself a sheep,
> The virgin up in Overlook,
> Cried herself to sleep.

> Oh, Susannah,
> Oh, don't you cry no more,
> The fellas up in Overlook
> Will even up the score.

We laughed, and even in the dark of the van I could see the puzzled look on Elizabeth's face and wondered if I'd have to explain it to her later.

"Too bad we don't have any sheep up here," said Joe.

"Yeah," said Ross. "Even a motherly goat would do."

"A chicken, even," said Andy.

"A *chicken*?" the guys all said, and we laughed.

Elizabeth gave me a questioning look.

"Don't ask," I whispered.

The minibus came out of the woods on an open stretch, and Phil suddenly pulled over to the side of the road. "Look at the stars!" he said.

We all piled out. For five or six minutes we stood leaning against the bus, looking up, Sue leaning back against Phil, his arms around her.

"This is where we should come in August when the Perseid meteor shower comes along," said Sue. "I don't think I've ever seen a sky so bright. There must not be any cloud cover at all."

I don't know what made me say what I did or why I was the one to break the silence then, but I heard myself saying, "I wonder if Dad and Sylvia are looking at these stars."

There was another moment of silence, and then Andy said, "Who?"

"My dad's getting married next month," I said.

"Ah!" said Phil.

"To her seventh-grade English teacher," Elizabeth explained. "They've been an item for several years, and it's been quite a romance. With a little help from Alice."

Then I had to tell them about how I'd invited Sylvia Summers to the Messiah Sing-Along without Dad knowing and how he'd won her away from our vice principal, Jim Sorringer, by writing such wonderful love letters when she went to England on a teacher-exchange program.

We talked about love all the way back to camp, about how it must feel to be married to the same person for forty or fifty years.

"I don't know," Phil said, turning to smile at Sue. "I think I could stand that quite well."

I realized that Pamela hadn't said anything for a long time, and I could have kicked myself for bringing up a subject that reminded her of her folks.

And then the bus was pulling into the wooded drive of Camp Overlook, and it was time to go back to our cabins.

When Gwen and I went inside ours to relieve Marsha, another full counselor who was taking over till we got back, we found the Coyotes still awake.

When Marsha had gone, Estelle asked, "So did you kiss?"

"Kiss? Kiss who?" asked Gwen.

"Anybody!" said Estelle. "Did you kiss any boys?"

"Only frogs," Gwen teased. "Did *you*?"

"Kiss *boys*?" Mary asked. And immediately the cabin was filled with cries of denial and disgust.

"So what *did* you do?" I asked.

"Saw a movie and had an ice-cream party," said Kim.

"And Josephine threw up," Mary announced.

"On your bed," Ruby added, looking at me.

*Great!* I thought as I pulled off the cover and threw it into the corner. Gwen and I took off our clothes in the dark, but I can always sense the girls watching. Latisha noticed the black underwear.

"Why you got on those pants?" she asked Gwen.

"'Cause I felt like it," Gwen said.

It was like living on stage each night, undressing in front of those girls. Even in the dark.

I don't know what it was—whether it was because all the junior counselors had gone out the night before so that the usual bedtime ritual was different or what—but Latisha was out of sorts all weekend. Despite the truce they'd made, the promise of friendship, she and Estelle fought constantly, and if Latisha wasn't arguing with Estelle, then it was anyone who got in her way. Kim seemed afraid of her and kept close to Gwen and me. My idea of having a group of close-knit girls was evaporating day by day.

"Latisha, knock it off!" I scolded her at dinner on Sunday when she kept bumping her arm against Ruby's, insisting that Ruby was taking up too much room.

"Okay," Latisha said, and promptly knocked Ruby's plastic water glass to the floor.

We studied her. "The mop is in the kitchen. Go get it," Gwen said.

Latisha simply folded her arms over her chest and sat with her lower lip protruding, glaring at us both.

"The mop, Latisha," I said.

She shook her head and refused. Ruby was all for going to get the mop herself for harmony's sake, but we wouldn't let her. Ruby would lie down on the floor and let people walk on her if we allowed it. Don't-Rock-the-Boat Ruby, we called her in our twice-weekly staff sessions.

When we got back to the cabin later, we held a conference to decide what Latisha's punishment should be.

"I think she ought to get her black ass whipped," said Estelle.

Latisha turned her glare on her.

"She shouldn't have any breakfast," said Mary.

"Shut your mouth," said Latisha.

It was obvious that anything we told Latisha she had to do, she would refuse, so we decided that for the remainder of the week, the evening server at the dining table would go to the kitchen to bring back food for everyone but Latisha. She would have to go to the kitchen and get her own unless she apologized to Ruby.

Latisha only shrugged. "So what?" she said.

But by the next night, as food was passed around the table to all but her, she was clearly getting angrier and angrier.

We brought it up at staff session.

"Seems to me you're handling it okay," Jack said. "You can't let her behavior go without consequences."

But on Tuesday night, when the girls were taking their showers, we realized that Latisha was missing.

"Who was the last one in here tonight?" I asked the other girls. "Mary, did Latisha follow you and Josephine to the showers?"

"I think so," said Mary.

"Can't you remember?"

"She was behind us when we left the cabin. I don't know if she came inside or not."

"Latisha?" I called over the rush of the water. "Latisha?" I called up at the high open window above.

No answer.

"I'll go," I told Gwen. Quickly retracing my

steps to the cabin, I half expected to find Latisha sitting defiantly on her bunk, refusing to shower with the rest of the girls. But the cabin was empty.

I immediately headed for the dining hall and the office. Connie was standing in the doorway talking to Richard and his dad.

"I can't find Latisha," I said breathlessly, my hair damp on my forehead. I told them how long we thought she'd been missing.

A missing camper at Camp Overlook is a red alert. Jack immediately set out for the overlook with a search lantern and gave another to Richard and me, instructing us to go to the river. Connie said she would check the cabins one by one and get more counselors searching if we didn't find Latisha right away.

"I'm scared," I confided to Richard as we headed down to the river. "I just can't see how she could slip away like that. I'm sure she was with us before we left for the showers." My voice was shaking.

"She upset about anything?" Richard asked. He's tall and lanky, very much like his dad. Probably got the longest neck of any boy I ever knew.

"Latisha's always upset about something. Her nose has been out of joint ever since we went into town the other night and someone else was in charge of our cabin. Then she was punished for knocking Ruby's glass on the floor in the dining hall. All you have to do is look at Latisha cross-eyed and she's mad."

"Well, we always check the river and the over-look first," Richard said. "We've found that the kids usually go to someplace familiar. She's not likely to go off in the woods by herself, but you never know. My guess is that she's hiding out in someone's cabin. It's too scary to go very far alone. Unless . . ." He stopped.

"Unless what?"

"Oh . . . unless she's suicidal or something, which I doubt." He grabbed my hand in the dark-ness because the path was rough, but I'm sure he knew that my heart was in my mouth. The lanterns they use at night in camp are really strong, and we could make out the riverfront even before we got there.

"No matter what I do for her, it's never enough," I said, my words coming fast. "And punishing her the other night must have seemed like proof posi-tive that we don't like her."

"We've got a kid like that in our cabin," Richard said. "Kids who grow up without love—well, they can't get enough, you know? Sometimes I think every kid should have a dog. A dog'll love you no matter what."

We walked along the riverbank, up and down, but there was no sign of Latisha, either sitting under a tree or floating in the water. That much, I guess, was fortunate.

"If anything's happened to her . . . ," I said, feeling more and more responsible. Then, "You don't think someone would come into camp and kidnap her, do you? Grab one of the kids?"

"Very unlikely," Richard said, and gripped my hand all the harder.

When we got back to camp, Connie hadn't found Latisha either, and the whole camp went on a "missing person alert." The outdoor lights came on, and all the children were instructed to stay on their bunks and be accounted for. Every full counselor and assistant counselor was given an area to check.

Gwen and I searched the picnic area.

"Do you think she's trying to walk back home?" I asked finally.

"Don't go off the deep end, Alice," Gwen said. "She's as clever as she is angry. We'll find her." We'd been looking now for twenty minutes, however, and no one had found her yet. We went back to our cabin more frightened than ever.

And then Mary and Josephine had to go to the bathroom, and they were the ones who made the discovery.

"Latisha!" the girls bellowed together, and Gwen and I came running.

Josephine would use only the stall that didn't have a lock on it because she was afraid she might not be able to get out. When she'd swung the door open, she told us, there was Latisha, standing up on the toilet seat, hidden behind the door. *We* could have looked, *should* have looked, not just taken a cursory glance under each door, looking for feet.

All I could do was put my arms around Latisha and hug her to me. I didn't have any voice to scold. And strangely enough, this time Latisha hugged back.

# 8

# News from
# Silver Spring

The next morning dawned dark and gloomy, and we had crafts in the big dining hall, while rain pattered down outside, spilling out the rainspouts and drumming on the roof. All the doors and windows were open, so the humid air brought with it the faint odor of mustiness and mildew, typical summer camp. The kids were working on making little baskets out of twigs, which they could then fill with small treasures found here at Overlook—pine cones and such—and take them with them when they left for home.

Mary had told me that Josephine was sick, so I'd taken her to the camp nurse, but it turned out that her temperature was normal, and the sickness seemed to be a figment of Mary's imagination. When I got Josephine back to the dining hall, Gwen had a second project in progress.

One of the tables was covered with newspaper,

and Gwen had about six different colors of paint in little containers in the center of the table. They were various shades of white, brown, black, yellow, orange, and red.

Each girl, Gwen said, was to take some of the paint and put it on her saucer. She was to keep mixing different colors until she matched the color of her own skin.

"Huh?" said Estelle. "I'm white. You're black."

"Really?" said Gwen, sitting down beside her. "Let's see."

Gwen put some black paint on her saucer, then smeared some on her arm. There was a great contrast between the pecan brown color of her skin and the paint.

"Now let's try you," she said, and put white on Estelle's saucer. Estelle smeared white on her arm, and of course it didn't match at all.

The Coyotes were engrossed in the project, and each began experimenting. Latisha and Ruby started out with brown paint, but it was much too dark. Mary and Josephine and Estelle started out with white paint, and it was much too white. Kim, strangely, chose orange as her color, but it didn't match any better than the others. Just to be different, I took red.

"You look like a ghost!" Latisha said to Estelle.

Silently, Estelle mixed some yellow into the

white paint on her saucer, then tried that on her arm. No match.

"You've gotta add some of *that*!" Kim said, pointing to the brown. Estelle mixed in a bit of brown. Better. She mixed in some more. Better still.

"Hey, look! I'm an Indian!" said Mary, making red stripes on her arm.

Several kids from a nearby table came over to watch. I looked at Gwen in admiration. She hadn't said a word. She had merely put out the paints, and every girl at the table learned that each of us is made up of a lot of different colors.

Connie was impressed. "Did you think this one up on your own, Gwen?" she asked.

"No. It's a project we did at summer Bible school," said Gwen.

"Well, I'm going to remember this one with my next load of campers," Connie told her. "I'm glad you're on board, Gwen."

So was I.

We lost the war with Latisha, though. Because lunch was served buffet style, everyone helped himself, and by evening we were back to our usual dinner routine, one runner serving the whole table, Latisha included. Gwen and I were too tired to carry it further. We knew we hadn't handled it well, but we didn't want her disappearing again.

"We can't win them all, and we can't reach them

all, either," Gwen told me. "If we do a good job with the others, we'll just have to accept that five out of six isn't bad."

A farm nearby allowed Camp Overlook to bring the children over a few times each summer to ride horses. So we marched the kids over there Wednesday afternoon, hiking across a high, breezy pasture, the campers exclaiming and jumping over cow pies, but I was surprised at the number who declared they'd never get on a horse. What surprised me even more was my own reluctance.

I'd never been on horseback, never been on a farm, really. Horses were something I saw from a distance. But suddenly here we were, standing at a fence, as six or seven horses were led out of a barn and saddled up. Richard rode one over to the fence and it seemed far larger than I had expected. When it rolled its eyes and snorted and chomped down on the bit, Josie gave a cry and dived behind my legs, and even Latisha vowed she wouldn't ride.

Connie walked alongside the horse as it moved down the line of campers. She told them its name—Soldier—and held up some of the braver children to stroke its side, but all it took was a toss of the head from Soldier and the kids cowered again. Only a dozen or so said they were willing to get on.

"It doesn't matter if you've never been on a horse," said Connie to the kids. She looked around at the assistant counselors. "Where's an assistant counselor who has never been on a horse. Doris? Tommie?"

I raised my hand, thinking I would be in the majority, and was suddenly horrified to discover I was the only one. No! They had to be lying! How could it be that I'd reached the age of fifteen and was the only one here who hadn't been on horseback? I quickly lowered my hand. Did ponies count? Ponies at a fairground? But I wasn't even sure I'd done that. A merry-go-round! Yes! I'd ridden a merry-go-round!

But then I heard Connie say, "Okay, Alice. Come right in here. We're going to start you out with Richard." I shrank back, shaking my head, and then I heard Estelle say, "Just tell her you're not gonna do it, Alice. You don't have to!" And then I knew I had to.

The farmer opened the gate so I could get through. I was trying to smile and swallow at the same time. He walked me over to Soldier, who lifted one hoof impatiently and put it down again with another toss of his head. What if he bit me? What if he kicked?

"The kids will feel safer if they can ride along with someone," Connie said, "so we're going to put you up there with Richard and show them how it's done."

Richard smiled down at me and moved back a little in the saddle. He slipped one foot out of the stirrup so I could use it to hoist myself up.

"Here you go," the farmer said, and I awkwardly swung my other leg over the horse, almost hitting Richard in the chest. Then I was in the saddle in front of him, and his arms were on either side of me, holding the reins.

"Just relax," Richard said as we moved forward. "He's really very gentle."

Connie was giving instructions, explaining how you tell a horse to go, to stop, to turn, to trot. I focused on Soldier's ears, the way they raised, then flattened, then twitched, as though he could understand everything we said. *How do you tell a horse that you're scared half out of your mind? To be merciful?*

Just as I was getting used to the feel of the horse beneath me, the heat of its body soaking into my thighs and calves, I could feel Richard make some slight movement and Soldier began to trot.

"Oh!" I said, startled.

"It's okay," Richard said into my hair. "Just hold on to the saddle."

But my fingers dug into his thighs like claws, and I was afraid to let go. My spine felt so stiff against Richard's chest, I was afraid I'd push him backward, but I couldn't help myself.

"Trust me," came his voice. It was all that was left to do. I held on as we went once around the paddock, and then the horse slowed to a walk, and it was someone else's turn to feel their insides turn to jelly. Richard brought Soldier to the gate again, and I slid off. Other campers stepped forward, and other horses were put into use.

"You did good, Alice!" Ruby said.

"Yeah! I thought he was going to buck!" said Mary.

"Was it fun?" asked Latisha.

"It was an adventure," I said, perspiration trickling down from my armpits.

"Well, maybe I'll go next week," Latisha told us.

We were coming back from the baseball diamond on Friday when I saw Lester outside the office, talking with Connie, hands in his pockets. Actually, Pamela saw him first.

"Studly!" she cried. That's what Pamela calls every guy who looks sexy to her.

Actually, he looked as though he'd been digging ditches, because he was windblown and sweat-stained. Handsome, nonetheless.

"Gwen, can you take over for me?" I asked.

"Tell him to stick around so we can see him too," said Pamela.

Lester pulled one hand out of his jeans' pocket and waved when he saw us, smiling at me as I crossed the clearing, Kim sticking to my side.

"Who's that? Your boyfriend?" Estelle asked.

"My brother," I said.

Latisha gave a little whistle. "He good-looking, all right," she said, making Mary and Ruby laugh.

"This is a surprise!" I told Lester as Connie smiled and went back in the office, but my pulse was speeding up. Why had he driven all the way up here? Why hadn't he just called? There must have been something about my face that told him how anxious I was, because Lester held up one hand to stop me. "Hey! Nobody died," he said, which only told me that *something* had happened.

Gwen herded the Coyotes on by, practically peeling Kim away from me, and Pamela and Elizabeth took their own girls into the dining hall for their afternoon popcorn and lemonade.

I gave Lester a hug but studied his eyes when I backed off. "So?" I said.

"Relax, will you? I've been mountain biking. Met some buddies up here yesterday, and we rented a cabin and some bikes. Figured I was so close, I might as well drop by the camp and check it out on the way home."

"Spy on me, you mean." I laughed, steering him

over to a bench under an oak tree. I fanned myself with the hem of my T-shirt. "We just finished a baseball game. Let me cool off, and then I'll show you around. So what's happening back home?"

"Well, there is a bit of disappointing news. Sylvia . . ."

I stopped fanning. "*What?*"

"Sylvia . . ."

"She *didn't*! She broke their engagement?"

"No, Al!"

"She's been in an accident?"

"Al, will you please shut up for five seconds? Her sister is very ill in Albuquerque, and Sylvia's flying out there. The wedding's been postponed."

"Oh, Lester! *No!*"

"I'm afraid so. Dad's pretty disappointed, as you can guess, but he agrees there's nothing else to do. Nancy was in the hospital for a bowel operation, and she's developed septicemia. Blood poisoning. It can be really serious."

"How can she be having a bowel operation? She's supposed to be Sylvia's maid of honor!"

"Tell that to her bowels. She didn't plan it, Al."

"But how long will Sylvia be gone?"

"Till her sister's out of danger and recovering, I imagine."

"But . . . but that could be a long time! Sylvia and Dad could have the wedding, and *then* she could go to Albuquerque! Lester, she and Dad were *this close* to getting married! First she goes to England. Now she's going to Albuquerque. Doesn't she care anything about Dad's feelings? Doesn't she—"

"Al," Les said sternly, "grow up."

I stopped cold. "What?"

"You're talking like an eight-year-old."

"But it's *true!* Dad will be so hurt! If it's going to take a long time for her sister to get better, they could get married and go on their honeymoon, and *then* Sylvia could take care of her!"

"Her sister could die."

I stared at Lester. "It's . . . it's that serious?"

He nodded. "And what kind of honeymoon do you think they would have with Sylvia worried constantly about Nancy?"

"What kind of wedding will they have if Nancy *dies*?" I countered. My shoulders slumped and I sat with my legs apart, arms dangling between my knees. "I was all set to be her bridesmaid. She took my measurements and everything!"

"So is this about your feelings or Sylvia's?"

I felt like crying, but I saw Craig and Ross glance at me from across the clearing, and Lester's admonition to grow up kept the tears back, I guess.

I sighed instead. "Is there anything I can do? Does Dad want me to come home now?"

"No, not at all. He's driving Sylvia to the airport this afternoon, and I told him I'd look in on you while I was up here—make sure the guys were treating you with respect."

I kicked his foot and we laughed. It felt good to laugh about *something*.

"They're really nice," I said. "The assistant counselor's part is hard, though. It's *work* keeping track of the kids, but the guys are fun."

"*How* much fun?" Lester said, raising one eyebrow.

"Well," I teased, "for one thing, we went swimming one night, and the guys were naked."

"Whoa!" Lester said, and looked at me hard.

"The girls had their clothes on, though."

"Yeah? Paint me a picture," Les said.

So I told him how we had sat on the boys' clothes and how the guys had come out and thrown us in. I wanted to tell him just enough to make him nervous but not enough to make him worry. Then Elizabeth and Pamela came out of the dining hall and sauntered over.

"Hi, handsome," Pamela said, sitting down next to Lester so that their thighs touched. She's shameless.

"Hey! How's it going?" he asked her.

"Great!" said Elizabeth. "The boys are terrific!"

"Yeah?" said Les.

"We went to a bar the other night," Pamela told him.

"A *restaurant*," I corrected. "We didn't drink, Lester, and an older counselor drove. It was pure, wholesome fun."

"I'll bet," said Lester.

"You don't have to worry about a thing," said Pamela. "Besides, Elizabeth brought condoms."

"Pamela!" Elizabeth yelled.

Lester looked at her, then at me.

"They're for Pamela," I said.

"Alice!" cried Pamela.

Lester looked around. "I take it there *is* adult supervision up here?"

"Yes, Lester. We're perfectly fine." I turned to Pamela and Elizabeth. "Sylvia's sister is sick and the wedding's been postponed. She's flying to Albuquerque this afternoon."

"Oh, Alice!" they said together.

"It's not the end of the world," I told them, trying to summon a little maturity. "I guess it will be a fall wedding. Whenever Nancy gets better, that is. . . ."

"So, are you going to show me around?" Les asked.

"Sure." I jumped up and grabbed his arm. The

kids were all in the dining hall now having their snack, so Pamela and Elizabeth went with us. We showed Lester the river and the canoes, the paths in the woods, and then Pamela and Elizabeth went back to the dining hall while Les and I walked to the overlook.

It was a really gorgeous afternoon—not too hot—and we could see layers of mountains, fading as clouds moved by, then coming into focus again. Les put his arm around me, and this time I felt the tears coming.

"I . . . f-feel so sorry for Dad," I gulped.

"So do I. But it will all work out, Al. When you've got somebody to share your troubles, it's a lot easier. He still has Sylvia, you know." And then, realizing that I didn't have a boyfriend, he said, "And even if you *don't* have somebody special, you—"

"Cool it, Lester. I'm not about to jump off the overlook because Sylvia postponed the wedding," I said.

He laughed and gave my waist a little tug. "Okay. Let's talk about you. What's the deal about the condoms?"

"Elizabeth brought some," I said. And added, laughing, "A ribbed Trojan with a lubricated tip."

Lester choked. *"Elizabeth?"*

I grinned. "She said they're for Pamela, except

she gave them to Gwen, and I don't know who has them now."

"You're not sharing *condoms,* are you?"

"Les, I'm not even having sex. Relax."

"Whew!" he said. "Okay. I'm relaxed. It *is* a nice place up here. I hope you're having a good time."

"I am. I'm glad I came."

We walked back and I introduced him to a few of the guys. Then Les talked a few minutes with Jack Harrigan, and finally he drove away.

There's mail call every day at three o'clock, and I went up to the office to see if I got something. I didn't. There was an envelope for Pamela, though. If any one of the assistant counselors needed a letter, I thought, it was Pamela. First her mom got everyone upset by leaving the family, and then she got them upset by saying she wanted to come back. Pamela seemed not to even want to think about it.

"Hey, Pamela! For you!" I said, waving the letter, and sat down beside her on the steps. As soon as she saw the postmark, though, her face clouded up. I looked the other way while she read it.

"Guess who's coming to town," Pamela said, crumpling up the letter into a tight little ball, then angrily squeezing it again for good measure.

"I don't know," I said, hesitating.

"Mom."

I studied her for a moment. "She really is, then! She wrote you from Colorado? How did she get the address up here?"

"Who knows? She finds out everything."

"When is she coming?

"She doesn't say. I don't want to be around when she shows up," Pamela said determinedly. "Let me stay at your place or something when she does, Alice! There'll probably be a big scene, and I just don't think I could take it. I can't understand why she'd even want to come back if Dad doesn't love her anymore."

"You don't think . . . maybe . . . they could work things out?"

"It's too late for that. It's been too long. Dad hates her."

We were both quiet for a minute or two.

"What do you *want* to happen?" I asked finally.

"I just want it *over*, one way or another. I hate this waiting around, wondering what will happen next. I either want them together or I want them apart."

I thought how often I'd felt something like that for the past couple of years about Dad and Sylvia. Except I'd never wanted them apart. I'd *always* wanted them to be together.

# 9

# Going Coed

That night, *our* night, none of the older counselors was available to drive us into town, so the six of us girls decided to sneak down to the river early and go skinny-dipping, just to say that we had. Doris, who felt she was on the verge of a cold, didn't want to go in but said she'd be our lookout.

"We'll just take a short swim before the guys start looking for us," Pamela said with a giggle. But we were all secretly hoping that the guys would find out where we'd gone and . . . Well, who knows what we were hoping. Just for something exciting to happen, I guess.

We weren't foolish enough to leave our clothes on the bank, though. We wadded them up and stuck them in the fork of a low tree. When we got down to our underpants, we wore them to the water's edge, then gave them to Doris to put in the tree for us, and dived in. Elizabeth refused to take off either her underpants or her bra, so there we were; one girl on the bank fully clothed; one girl in the water in her underwear; and four girls in the river naked.

We swam quietly, giggling to each other, feeling very risqué. When the guys didn't come down right away, I noticed, none of us suggested we get out, even though the water was frigid and I could feel my teeth chattering. We just kept swimming around, watching the path to the dining hall. I noticed Pamela's voice getting a little louder, just in case the guys were within earshot. And soon, down the path they came—all six of the male assistant counselors.

What we did, of course, was shriek and duck down under the water, swimming a little downriver to pretend we weren't there, which was ridiculous. And then *they* were in the water, all their clothes on the bank, and after we got over being semi-embarrassed and silly, we just swam around and talked, and it seemed to me we were pretty grown-up, Gerald included.

"Was that your boyfriend or your brother I saw you with this afternoon?" Craig asked me.

"My brother. Les. My dad's wedding's been postponed because my new mom's sister is sick," I explained.

"Tough luck," said Craig.

"I'm going to feel so much better when they're finally married," I told him. "Dad's been waiting a long time."

"Yeah, sure," I heard Joe murmur, and the others laughed.

I didn't say any more about Dad and Sylvia. I didn't want people guessing about their private lives when they didn't even know them. So I just dog-paddled around, thinking how strange and exciting it felt to be swimming at night. The sky was cloudy, though, and we couldn't see much of anything except a ball of white somewhere back on the bank, which I realized, finally, was our ball of underwear in the fork of the tree.

Both Elizabeth and Pamela were swimming around Ross like sharks, I thought. Gwen and Joe were nuzzling off by themselves, G. E. was talking with Doris, who was sitting on an overturned canoe, and the rest of us were just floating about, enjoying a free swim without the little kids.

As I watched Gwen and Joe, though, who were now kissing, their lips and who knows what else locked together, I began to wonder if the directors of this camp knew what they were doing. We were running on hormones, everyone said, and here we were, away from home, totally naked, in the dark, and . . . Maybe they figured there was safety in numbers. G. E. slid into the water next.

There was a sudden rustling in the bushes, the quick thud of feet, and suddenly, with a loud "Hi-*yah*!" Jack Harrigan did a cannonball in the river, splashing everyone within ten yards. He was the only one besides Elizabeth and Doris *not* naked. Maybe the directors *did* know what they were doing.

"So how's the fishing?" he asked, and his voice held a grin.

"Not so good," Andy joked. "The babes aren't biting."

"Speak for yourself," came Joe's voice, and I heard Gwen laugh.

"Maybe you're using the wrong bait," said Richard's dad.

"Hey, we've got a river, a breeze, a night, a moon . . . ," said Ross.

"No moon," said Andy.

"Okay, skip the moon. But . . ."

With the guys talking to Richard's father, we girls felt it was safe to swim downstream, sneak out, and get our clothes. Doris had retrieved our bundle of underpants from the tree and brought them down to a row of bushes, then went back to get the rest of our pants and shirts. We climbed out, one after the other, and dressed.

"Darn!" said Pamela. "Just when things were heating up."

"Ross kissed me!" Elizabeth whispered excitedly.

"How could you tell who it was? It was dark," said Pamela, and she didn't sound pleased.

"I think he was going around kissing everyone," I said, trying to defuse a potential quarrel. "Somebody touched me underwater."

"Probably Gerald," said Elizabeth, to take *me* down a peg or two.

"It's going to be hard to go back home with Mom and Dad hovering around all the time, knowing where I am every living minute," said Elizabeth, zipping up her jeans.

"Everyone should be so lucky," said Tommie.

"Lucky how?"

"Most of these kids don't have anyone to hover."

"I guess so," said Elizabeth. "Just the same, tonight was really fun."

"Till Richard's dad showed up, anyway," said Pamela. "I suppose Richard's the establishment spy."

"I don't think so," I said. "He's too nice."

"Then how else did his dad know to come swimming with us? *Some*body must have told him that the guys were swimming nude last week," said Tommie.

Suddenly I remembered.

"*Lester!*" I cried. "*He* was talking with Jack Harrigan before he left."

"Kill him for us," said Pamela.

. . .

I felt the need to call home. I was going to give Lester a piece of my mind, for one thing, but what I really wanted was to hear Dad's voice and find out how he was doing. I went to the office later that night and dialed. The phone rang so many times, I was afraid I'd get the answering machine, but then Dad picked it up.

"Dad? Did I wake you?" I asked. "Did you go to bed early?"

"Alice! No, I was just sitting out on the porch. How are you, honey?"

"How are *you*, Dad? I'm really sorry about Sylvia's sister."

"Well, so am I. It was a big disappointment for both of us, but there's nothing to be done. Nancy's seriously ill. Septicemia is a worrisome business, and we're just hoping she pulls through okay."

"Can't the doctors do something? Give her antibiotics?"

"Well, of course. That's what they're doing. But it's tricky. They have to figure out just what combination of drugs will work. Meanwhile, the infection can spread to the brain, the heart—almost anywhere."

"Oh, Dad. You've waited so long."

"I can wait a bit longer, I guess. Right now the important thing is Nancy's health."

"Is Sylvia coming back to teach in the fall?"

"Everything depends on Nancy. Sylvia's already told the principal she probably won't be here for the start of school. We'll just have to wait and see."

We were both quiet for a few seconds. "I wish I was there," I said finally.

"Now, Alice, what could you do? You are exactly where you are supposed to be, and I hope you're having a good time. Are you?"

"Well, yes. I didn't know that being an assistant counselor was so exhausting, though. I mean, I'm tired even when we don't do anything physical. Just trying to keep the peace wears me out."

He laughed, and it was good to hear that familiar chuckle. "Kids are a handful, all right," he said. "I can remember times you and Lester about drove me up the wall."

"Not recently, I hope."

"Not too recently, no."

"Has anyone asked about me? Called or anything?"

I could almost hear Dad's brain working at being tactful. Playing it safe. Trying to decipher what I was really asking.

"I think most of your friends know you're away, hon," he said. "There aren't any phone messages. I don't know about e-mail. Everything going okay there at camp? You and Gwen hitting it off as cabin mates?"

"Gwen's wonderful," I said. "Pamela and Elizabeth are in separate cabins, thank goodness, because they both like the same guy—there are a *lot* of cute boys here—but other than that, we're doing okay." I didn't want to get into the nude swimming bit.

"Well, you'll be home in another week, right?" he said. "Call when you get in. I don't know who will pick you up, but somebody will drive over."

"Dad? Have you heard from Sylvia since she left?" I asked.

"Oh, yes. She's called twice—once after she got there and again from the hospital. Right now Nancy's holding her own, but we won't know anything much for a while. Sylvia's where she needs to be too, Al. That's life. We take things as they come."

He was saying all the right things, but how did he really *feel*?

"I love you, Dad," I said. "Rivers."

"I love you too, Al. Oceans."

I had a hard time falling asleep that night. I kept thinking about Pamela and Elizabeth. We'd been friends for a long time, and I didn't want anything to come between the two of them. We'd come to camp excited and looking forward to three weeks of fun together. It had been that and even more for Elizabeth, but I'm not sure about Pamela. And the letter from her mother sure didn't help.

I got up finally, and, throwing on my jacket, I slipped out of the cabin and made my way down the narrow lane. Night noises were all around me, and a breeze rustled the leaves of the aspens. When I got to cabin twelve, I noiselessly opened the screen door and moved across the floor to Pamela's bunk. She was lying with her face to the wall.

"Pamela," I whispered.

At first she didn't move. Then she rolled over and peered at me through the darkness. "Alice?" she said. She stared at me for a moment, then scooted over to make room. I lay down on my side and rested my cheek on one hand.

"I'm worried about you and Liz," I said.

"Well, don't be."

"I just hate to see you fighting over some guy. Even Ross, nice as he is."

"We're not fighting." Her voice was flat. "This isn't the first time I've lost out. It won't be the last," she said, and she sounded resigned. Defeated.

I tried to see her face in the darkness. This was *Pamela* talking? The talented, sexy Pamela Jones whom I'd envied so much in sixth grade? Then I remembered how she had pulled out of the high school Drama Club last year because she figured she didn't have a chance at a lead part. Now *I* was worried.

"You know," I said, "if ever a girl needed to have a guy be loving and tender with her—a guy her own age—it's Elizabeth."

"I know that," Pamela whispered back. "I was lying here thinking the same thing. And it's not just tonight; I've been noticing how much he likes her. The way he watches her. When I'm feeling mature about it, I wish Ross lived closer so they could go out once camp's over. When I'm feeling sorry for myself, I'm glad he's in Philadelphia."

We were both quiet awhile.

"I hate to see you feeling so low," I whispered finally. "It's . . . it's partly your mom, isn't it?"

There was a catch in her voice. "I get sad thinking about how we used to be, when we were a family."

"I wish you'd consider yourself a part of *my* family for a while," I said. "I wish you felt you could come over whenever you wanted and talk to me and Dad."

I could hear a note of mischief creeping into her voice. "Lester, too?"

I knew Lester would kill me, but I said it anyway. "Sure. Just consider him your big brother. G'night, sis."

"Good night, Alice," she said.

# 10

# The Great Kelpie Hunt

On the Fourth of July, each cabin was given a flag to hang out front, and the camp held a picnic. We had relay races and potato sack races, and the full counselors performed in a makeshift band with a tin whistle, a potato chip can for a drum, a harmonica, and a washboard. We hand-cranked peach ice cream, and each kid had a chance to turn the handle.

I thought this might be something Latisha would particularly enjoy, but if Latisha enjoyed anything, she kept it to herself. Gwen and I saw a modest improvement in most of our girls. Ruby quit trying to smuggle food from the dining hall, which to us meant she was more comfortable here at camp—didn't feel as though there might not be enough food to go around. Kim was less fearful, Josephine more adventurous, Mary less protective. Even Estelle showed less prejudice toward

Ruby and Gwen and, to some extent, toward Latisha.

But Latisha was like a sphinx. If we saw a change at all, she was a bit more quiet, but not, it seemed, less angry. Some of the Coyotes had asked to make a second twig basket to take home to someone they loved. But Latisha showed no interest in making more. She enjoyed contact sports, anything that allowed her to bump or push or pull or wrestle. Otherwise, she sat on the sidelines and glowered at everyone else.

On our last Friday, assistant counselors' night out, the guys were planning to take us on the promised "Kelpie Hunt," led by Phil. It was supposed to be a preview of what our little campers would get the following night.

"You can never tell what the guys have up their sleeves," said Doris. "I think we ought to wear bathing suits under our shorts, just in case."

"Hey! How about *nothing* under our shorts? I'd like that better," said Pamela.

"I'm going to be sorry when camp's over," said Tommie. "I wish we had another week here. Craig and I were just starting to get chummy."

"You could always write," I said.

"Oh, you know how summer romances go," she told me.

Elizabeth was thoughtful. "Well, Ross and I

really like each other, and I wish ours would go on forever," she said. "You know who I feel sorry for?" I hoped she wouldn't say Pamela. "I feel sort of sorry for G. E. Why don't we each try to say something nice to him before camp's over? I mean, something spontaneous and sincere."

"Like what?" asked Gwen.

"Anything. That you like his T-shirt. Or just sit and talk with him a few minutes. We don't want him to know we agreed to do it, but it would give him something nice to remember about Camp Overlook. He must feel like the odd man out."

"He is the odd man out," said Doris.

"But you know how you'd feel if it were you," I said.

"I suppose we can manage to find something nice to say," said Tommie. "He's not a total dork in *every*thing."

When the kids had gone to the dining hall and the full counselors took over for the evening, we assistant counselors gathered at one of the trailheads, where the guys were whispering among themselves.

I was relieved to see that Phil was there, obviously in charge. Sue had said that the Kelpie Hunt had become a tradition, sort of an initiation for all the new assistant counselors, but you could tell that the guys knew what was coming and the girls didn't. It sounded like fun, though, and we went along with their joke—sort of like a haunted house at Halloween, except that the guys got to be the ghosts.

"O-*kay*!" Phil said. "Is everybody *ready*?" And the guys all grinned at us.

"For *what*, exactly?" asked Gwen.

"Here's the deal," Phil said mysteriously. "There's a creature here at Camp Overlook that lives on the river bottom, and few have ever seen it. A kelpie is half ghost, half horse, and if it calls your name, you'll feel this irresistible compulsion to climb on its back, where it will take you down under the water and you'll never be seen again. *Our* job is to find the kelpie before it finds you."

"Great," said Pamela. "And which of you guys gets to play the kelpie?"

"Hey, ye of little faith!" said Richard. "It's an old Scottish superstition, but doesn't every superstition have something real behind it?"

"So what are we supposed to do?" asked Elizabeth. I noticed that Ross was standing behind her with his arms wrapped around her, face against her cheek. Elizabeth was stroking his hand.

Phil continued: "Well, the kelpie knows you're here. It knows everything about us—who's here, who leaves. We'll try to spot it when it comes to the surface for air—capture it, if we can. If you hear it, of course, you have to go toward it. The trick is to keep from climbing on its back. That's what the guys are here for, to protect you."

"Yeah, sure," we said, laughing. "And if it calls *your* name?"

The guys all looked at Phil.

"Oh, it's gender-specific," Phil said. "It only calls girls' names."

We laughed again and set off—some of the guys in front of us, some behind, with only the small beam of Phil's flashlight to guide us. We figured that Gerald must have been assigned the role of the kelpie, because he wasn't with us.

"Why are we going uphill if the kelpie's in the river?" I asked.

"To throw him off guard," said Richard, and the boys whispered some more.

We continued climbing, the guys holding back branches that would have scratched our faces, until finally we came out on a ridge in the moonlight. I hadn't been on this trail or this ridge, but I could tell by the way the wind tossed my hair that we were up pretty high. There didn't seem to be anything between us and the sky.

"What we've got to do," said Phil, stopping, "is rappel down the cliff, where the kelpie would least expect us."

"In the dark?" asked Doris.

"How far down is it?" asked Elizabeth.

"Only fifty feet or so."

Several of us gasped at once. *Isn't there any adult supervision up here?* Lester had asked when he'd visited. I wondered how old Phil was— twenty-two, maybe? Still . . .

And then we heard a faraway call. "Pam-e-la! . . . Pam-e-la!" Gwen and I smiled at each other. We figured one of the guys here had a cell phone or a walkie-talkie; how else could the call come just as we'd reached the top?

"Uh-oh," said Andy. "I'll be brave. I'll go with her."

We jeered.

"Strange, but I don't feel the slightest urge to go toward it," Pamela said. "I think the kelpie's losing its magic."

"You don't fool around with a kelpie," said Andy. "You sure don't want it coming looking for *you.* C'mon."

"Watch it, Pamela," said Craig.

"If it's a choice between Andy and the kelpie, take the kelpie," said Ross.

Phil produced a couple of harnesses and ropes that seemed to be tied to a tree, just waiting for us. I couldn't believe Pamela was actually going to do it, but she gamely stepped forward and put her feet through the straps of the harness, pulling it up around her.

"I think all the *guys* should go fight the kelpie and we'll stay up here," said Doris.

"Yeah, me too," said Tommie.

"Oh, that wouldn't work. We have to have bait to catch a kelpie, and he's partial to girls," said Richard.

I began to get a panicky feeling in my chest. This was dangerous. Was this one of those times Lester had warned me about, when you have to use common sense and say no?

In the moonlight Phil was demonstrating to Pamela how you hold the rope to rappel yourself down the side of a cliff.

"Pam-e-la! . . . Pam-e-la!" the faraway voice called again.

"We'll go together," said Andy, getting in the second harness. In a matter of minutes Pamela and Andy dropped over the edge, and all we could hear were their feet scuffling along the face of the cliff. Then suddenly, eerily, all was quiet.

As the moon went behind a cloud, then emerged again, Phil stood with one finger to his lips, listening, waiting. Then he and Richard began to pull on the two ropes, and after a while the harnesses came up over the edge, minus Pamela and Andy.

"Al-ice! . . . Al-ice!" came the call.

Suddenly I could feel my body trembling. I didn't know if I was going to be sick or faint, but I just crouched down, my hands over my stomach. I felt Richard's arm around me as he crouched down too.

"Hey!" he said. "You're shaking!" And then he put his mouth to my ear. "It's safe," he said. "Trust me."

I thought of all the stories I'd heard about guys talking girls into stuff they shouldn't do. Girls getting into cars with guys who were stoned. Was I about to rappel myself over the edge of a fifty-foot drop in a flimsy harness to my death? But no one here was drunk. No one was stoned. Phil was the head counselor, and Richard had kept me safe on the horse. I decided to trust.

"You'll love it," said Craig.

I got up shakily. "That's what they all say," I told him. "Will you still respect me in the morning?" Everyone laughed.

They helped me into one of the harnesses while Richard got in the other. Then, side by side, we were lowered over the edge. I was breathing so fast, I wondered if my heart would give out. What a coward I was! First the horse, and now this!

"Al-ice! . . . Al-ice!" came the voice from below.

I let myself down a little more, a little more, almost glad for the darkness so I couldn't see the river. All of a sudden Richard grabbed hold of my rope and swung me over beside him. I gave a small shriek, afraid we'd both go crashing down. But all he said in my ear was, "Shhhh. Don't make a sound."

And the next thing I knew, my feet were on solid ground. We couldn't have traveled more than ten feet.

In the moonlight I could see Pamela and Andy grinning at me, fingers to their lips. I looked around and stepped out of the harness. The "cliff" was only a high bank over a hill below. The real drop was a lot farther on, but in the dark, from above, we couldn't see that. I put my hands to my face and suppressed a giggle.

"Tom-mie! . . . Tom-mie!" the voice came, and I sat down in the wet grass beside Pamela as we waited for all the girls' names to be called, wondering how many times this trick had been played on the assistant counselors—the girl counselors—at Camp Overlook. Had the guys decided in advance who was pairing off with whom? I wondered as we waited for Tommie to come down. But it was great fun, scary as anything, and when all the girls were down, we were allowed to talk again. We hooted and laughed at ourselves.

"Alice was hyperventilating," said Pamela. "I could hear her all the way down the bank."

"I was afraid she'd pass out on me," said Richard.

I think Elizabeth was having the best time of all. It was hard to see her and Ross in the dark, but whenever they stepped into moonlight, they were together. They didn't hug or kiss in front of the little campers when they were on duty, but I would see their hands touch momentarily, the smile that passed between them, the softening of Elizabeth's face when she watched him, and it almost made me want to stand up and shout, *Yes!* Here in the woods, though, they didn't have to hide how they felt about each other.

It was a long way down on the path to the river, but our ordeal wasn't over yet. Halfway there, Phil stopped us again.

"Okay, we've come to a tunnel," he said, "and we'll have to crawl through one at a time."

By now I was feeling more confident of myself. If I could ride a horse, I could rappel down a bank. If I could rappel down a bank, I could crawl through a tunnel. So I volunteered to be first in line after Phil, Pamela behind me. I wedged my body through the narrow opening on my hands and knees, feeling quite sure we were simply between two large boulders. I bet we could easily have walked around them, but this time I felt certain I was up to it.

Halfway through, though, one strap of my overalls came loose and, dangling between my legs as I crawled, caught its buckle on something. I couldn't go backward or forward, and the space was so narrow that I couldn't maneuver my arms to reach it.

"You coming?" Phil called over his shoulder.

"What's the matter?" asked Pamela, bumping into me from behind.

"I'm stuck!" I yelped. "My buckle's caught on something."

"Can you reach it?" Phil asked.

"No."

"I'll help you," he said.

"No!" I insisted. "Pamela, you've got to do it."

We were both wrestling with the strap, her hands between my legs, with scarcely enough room to move our arms, while somebody else bumped into Pamela. All we could do was laugh. It's a wonder we got me loose at all.

Free at last, we were still laughing about it when we reached the river, but there was the kelpie—someone with a huge rubber horse mask, complete with mane, swimming about in the water. Of course he came charging out as soon as he saw us, and of course a mock battle ensued, ending with all of us in the river. We had a great time.

"Hey, Gerald," I said when I noticed him sliding into the water. "You make a great kelpie."

"What do you mean?" he asked innocently. "I just got here. It's the guy with the horse's head you should be talking to."

"I mean the voice. Voice of the kelpie. You should work for Voice of America or something."

I could tell he was pleased.

The guys had brought sodas and chips, so we sat on the bank, talking and laughing and swatting at an occasional mosquito. The "kelpie," one of the older counselors, joined in. Phil and Craig told us stories of past Kelpie Hunts—the night even Phil had lost his way, for instance, and Jack Harrigan had to come looking for them.

Finally, though, we girls headed back to the showers to wash the river water from our hair. Pamela moved up behind Gwen and me. "Anybody see Elizabeth?" she asked.

I looked around. "She was with us all evening."

"Not on the bank, she wasn't," said Pamela. "At least I didn't see her."

We all stopped and looked about.

"What about the guys?" I asked. "Weren't they all there too?"

"All except Ross," said Tommie.

Pamela and I looked at each other. She didn't say a word; her face said it all.

# 11

# Girl Talk

We went on to the showers and took off our wet clothes. Even lukewarm water felt good to us after the cold of the river. I knew that the topic of conversation was going to be Elizabeth, but just that moment she walked in.

Her hair was tangled and there were leaves on the back of her T-shirt. Her face was flushed and she was breathless.

"Oh, *here* you are!" she said, as though *she* had been looking for *us*.

"Aha! She's got grass on her back!" said Tommie.

"Somebody check out Ross," Doris kidded.

"Naw. He'd have grass on his knees," said Gwen.

Elizabeth just took off her clothes and turned on a shower.

"Where did you go?" Pamela asked. "We've been wondering where you were."

"Ross and I went for a walk, that's all," Elizabeth said. She closed her eyes and turned her face up toward the spray.

The rest of us looked at each other and grinned.

"Uh-huh," said Tommie knowingly. "The way we figure, Liz, you've been missing for about forty-five minutes. Maybe longer."

"So it was a long walk," said Elizabeth, smiling.

But Pamela and I wouldn't let her off so easily.

"Well," I said, "what happened?"

"What do you mean? Nothing. We just talked."

"Elizabeth . . . !" said Pamela.

"Her cheeks are red," said Gwen.

"And getting redder," said Doris.

"You might as well tell us," Pamela teased, and I think she was beginning to enjoy it. "If you don't, we'll go ask Ross."

Elizabeth suddenly turned and faced us triumphantly. "Well," she said, "I *did* it."

There was no sound at all in the showers except running water. Pamela reached up and turned hers off, and we continued staring at Elizabeth as though she had just risen from the dead. *Elizabeth? Elizabeth* had done IT before any of the rest of us? Elizabeth *Price*?

*"Really?"* It was all I could think of to say.

"With Ross?" Tommie asked.

Still grinning stupidly, Elizabeth nodded.

"Elizabeth?" I said again, disbelieving. "*Really* really?" We were flabbergasted.

"Did you use a condom?" Gwen asked her.

Elizabeth blinked and stared back at us. "Not *that*!" she exclaimed.

I let out my breath. "*What,* then?"

Elizabeth smiled. "I . . . let him touch me."

Gwen rolled her eyes. "First base, second base, third base . . . *what*?"

"My breasts," Elizabeth whispered. I mean, for Elizabeth, this was major, *Major*!

She just kept on grinning. "I . . . I never let a guy do that before," she said.

Well, I hadn't either. Not even Patrick and I had done that.

"Details! Details!" I said. "Did you take off your bra or what?"

"I wasn't wearing one," said Elizabeth.

I turned my shower off too and wrapped my towel around me. Pamela and I sat Elizabeth down on the bench at one end of the room as Tommie and Doris and Gwen gathered around.

"Okay, slowly. One step at a time. You *planned* this?" I asked, really curious.

"Of course I didn't plan it. I didn't even know what we'd be doing on the Kelpie Hunt. I just knew it would be dark."

"And Ross . . . ?"

"He just invited me to go for a walk. And we kissed. And—"

"And . . . ? Don't stop, Elizabeth!" Pamela scolded.

"And he worked his hands up under my sweatshirt in back while he was kissing me, and . . . and when he discovered I wasn't wearing a bra . . . his hands came around and he touched me in front. And . . . I let him. I wanted him to."

We relived every second of it with Elizabeth.

"Is that all?" I asked finally.

"No. . . . Then he . . . he kissed them."

He *kissed* them?

"Kissed your breasts?" I asked. Oh, this was wild. I couldn't believe it!

Elizabeth just grinned.

Gwen gave an exaggerated, romantic sigh that broke the tension, and we laughed a little. "Hey, girl, you don't have to spill everything," she told Elizabeth. "You going to take us along on your wedding night?"

"It's just that . . . we promised once—Pamela and Elizabeth and I—that we'd tell each other everything," I explained.

"Ha! Not even guys do that, I'll bet. Only the parts that make them look good," said Doris.

"I don't think I should be telling you this," said Elizabeth, now that she'd told. "Ross said he wouldn't tell anyone."

"We won't ask any more," I said.

"There isn't any more to tell," Elizabeth said, and sighed happily.

We began talking about other things then, but I couldn't help remembering that only two years before on a train trip to Chicago, a man had touched one of Pamela's breasts, and Elizabeth had wanted her to go to a priest the next day and have it blessed. It was a different Elizabeth who sat rapturously now in the shower house, grinning still. I wondered what she'd tell the priest this time when she got home. Or if she would tell him anything at all.

Saturday was a day of "last times." The big canoe race, then our last lunch together, our last volleyball game, our last swim.

The hour before dinner was devoted to packing up, making sure all the campers were taking home everything they'd brought with them. And after dinner, while the kids watched cartoons, the assistant counselors were sent back to scour our cabins and see if we could find anything that remained unpacked that we wouldn't need in the morning. We looked under the bunks, behind the door, up on the rafters.

As we went back and forth to the trash can outside, throwing out broken shoelaces and pieces of pretzel and torn pages of comics, Tommie called over, "We should have some sort of ceremony—the six of us. Toss something in the river to show we'll return."

"Like the Bible says, 'Cast your bread upon the water'?" asked Doris.

"Huh?" said Pamela, coming down the lane from cabin number twelve.

"Well, something like that," said Tommie.

"We *should*!" said Elizabeth. "Flower petals or something!"

Gwen suddenly smiled. "What about a six-pack?"

"What?" I said. "A six-pack?"

She went inside our cabin and returned with the box of Trojans. While we gathered around in amusement, she tore open one end and took out six little foil wrapped condoms, dropping one in each of our hands.

"To the river!" she said, thrusting one fist in the air, and giggling, we set off.

At the water's edge each of us made a wish, then tossed her little foil-packet out into the river.

"I want to come back someday to Camp Overlook," said Tommie, tossing hers.

"I want to see Ross again," said Elizabeth, going next.

"I want to see *Joe* again!" said Gwen.

Doris thought for a minute. "I want to get through geometry next year." Out went her condom into the water.

I didn't have to think long about my wish. "I want Dad and Sylvia's wedding to finally come off this fall." I threw overhanded, and my condom sailed out way past the others.

Pamela was just drawing back her arm when Craig came down the path to secure the canoes.

"What's this? What's this?" he asked, squinting at the little foil packets that were bobbing about on the slow-moving current. Then he looked at the one in Pamela's hand. "Is that what I think it is?"

"Yeah," said Pamela. "An end to summer."

"Well, hey! Don't let it go to waste!" Craig said, trying to grab it from her.

Pamela threw. "It's all yours," she said.

"Have a good swim!" Gwen said with a laugh, as we turned and made our way up the bank.

"You didn't tell us what you wished," I said to Pamela.

"The same old," she said. "About my mom."

Saturday night, of course, started with the Kelpie Hunt for the young campers. It was a little different from ours. They could squeeze through "the tunnel" if they wanted, with plenty of light from the lanterns, but no one rappelled down a bank, and only the bravest, the most eager, heard their names called. The rest were closely guided by counselors, so that everyone got the excitement of going into the woods at night, but only a few confronted the beast head-on. And when they got to the river's edge, the counselor who played the kelpie let some of the boys pull off his horse mask so that all the kids knew it was a fun joke.

After our showers later we changed into our pajamas and had our last session around the campfire. It was a quiet, sentimental affair, with the campers clinging to their counselors, reluctant to let go. Some of them clung to each other, their newfound friends. Estelle had taken to Gwen, despite all her racist remarks, but Latisha seemed as aloof as ever. When I put an arm around her shoulder, her body was stiff, and she almost imperceptibly shrugged me off.

"I wish," Connie said at the campfire, "that I could send a little bit of Camp Overlook home with each of you. You all have your collection of pine cones, of course, and the twig baskets we made. But what I hope most is that you will take back the knowledge that there are a lot of people who are different from you in some way, and yet you can get along."

The campfire flickered on all the little faces that somberly stared into the flames.

"What we *especially* hope," Connie said, "is that you remember that of all the people there are in this world, there is only one you. Nobody else is exactly like you. You are special. In fact, it's your very differences from other people that make you *you*. Some of you came here thinking that you could never sleep away from home. You found out that you could. Some of you thought you could never go into a dark woods, or paddle a canoe, or ride a horse. You did. Some of you learned to swim while you were here. So right now I want you to turn to the campers sitting next to you and pat those people on the back."

The kids started laughing then and patted each other a little too hard, getting slaps on the back in return.

"And now," said Connie, "I want you to pat *yourselves* on the back."

This made the kids really whoop it up. They grabbed each other's hands to help them reach their own backs. There were a lot of "ow's" and "oof's," but almost everyone was smiling.

When they calmed down at last, Jack Harrigan took over and led the kids in the Camp Overlook cheer:

> "Clap your hands!
> Stamp your feet.
> Our Camp Overlook
> Can't be beat!"

We sang the camp song, then Connie read some poems, and after that the campers and counselors quietly, almost reverently, made their way back to their cabins, like deer going into the forest, as Connie always said.

Except that our Coyotes wanted to linger a while longer, and so did the girls from Doris and Pamela's cabin. So we all sat together on the logs, watching the flames die down in the bonfire, listening to the crackle and pop of the wood.

"Well," said Doris, "tomorrow at this time, you'll all be home again, and tonight will be just a memory. It will be a good one, though, won't it?"

"Yeah. I wish I *never* had to go home," said a girl from Pamela's cabin, and I wondered if Pamela didn't feel the same way.

"Me either," said Estelle.

"There's not a thing about home you've missed while you were here?" I asked. "Not a single thing?"

"I don't miss being made fun of because I can't read as good as my sister," said the girl named Virginia.

"I don't miss bein' hit upside my head 'cause Daddy say I shootin' off my mouth," said Latisha. "I wish I didn't *never* have to go see him."

We were all quiet for a moment.

"I'd just like to have something to miss," said another girl.

"And somebody to miss *me*," said Estelle.

I think that Gwen and Doris and Pamela and I all reacted to that the same way, because we put our arms around the nearest girls and pulled them toward us.

"*I'll* miss you," I said to Mary and Kim, trying to pull Estelle over as well.

"We'll miss you too," said Josephine.

Some of the girls went right to sleep when we reached our cabin, but others were reluctant to let go of the evening.

"Good night, everybody," came Josephine's sleepy voice from her bunk.

"Good night, Josie," said Ruby.

Kim, however, was weeping because she didn't want to say good-bye the next day.

"Hey, Kim! Your aunt's going to be waiting for you! And is she ever going to love that twig basket you made!" I said.

"But I don't want to leave *you*!" Kim wept.

"Shut up, girl," came Latisha's voice from above.

"Latisha," I said, "do you think that on this last night here at camp, you could manage to say something nice to Kim?"

There was silence. And then Latisha said, "Could you quiet down, Kim? I'm trying to sleep up here."

And for Latisha, I guess, that was progress.

# 12

# Home

It was strange. The kids were more subdued going home than they were going up to Camp Overlook. I would have thought it would have been the opposite.

"Hardly any of them knew each other on the way there, but they whooped it up like old friends," I said to Gwen.

"Whistling in the dark," she told me. "They were trying to hide their nervousness, that's all."

"And when you consider what most of them are going back to, there's not much to whoop about, I guess," said Elizabeth.

As we'd boarded the buses that morning outside the dining hall Ross had kissed her just before we got on. Ross's brother had driven down from Philadelphia to pick him up, so Ross and Elizabeth were saying their good-byes as we loaded the kids. Everyone was watching, but I don't think Elizabeth even cared.

True to our word, each of us assistant counselors managed to say something nice to Gerald.

"Hey, G. E.," I called as he stepped on his bus. "I'm going to listen for you on the evening news." He grinned.

We stopped halfway home to get the kids lunch at McDonald's, and when we got on the bus again, I sat next to Elizabeth. She was looking about as peaceful as I'd ever seen her, smiling to herself. I would have thought she'd be weeping.

"Must be having a Ross thought," I said.

"He's one of the nicest guys I've ever met," she murmured.

I settled in close to her, our shoulders touching. "What did you like most about him?"

She thought for a minute. "He . . . he just sort of let me come to him, you know? He didn't rush me."

"In other words, *you* put the moves on *him*."

She laughed. "Not exactly. It was just . . . well, a mutual thing."

"I guess that's the way love's supposed to be," I said. But I still couldn't figure why she wasn't more upset about leaving camp. Leaving Ross. I glanced over at her but didn't say anything. She was the one who put it into words:

"I know we may not see each other again. But just to know that . . . that there are guys *like* him . . . I mean, that I could feel the way I do about him. . . . Well, that's hopeful."

"Very," I said.

I had hoped, I guess, that Latisha would give some sign that she was sorry camp was over—that we had been kind to her, at least. But when she got off the bus, she saw someone waiting for her. She just gave us a shrug, and went over to him, dragging her bag behind her. It didn't look as though he said two words to her. They just walked over to his pickup, he tossed her bag in back, and they drove away.

"I wish . . . ," I began.

"I know," said Gwen.

Kim was the most affectionate, tearfully hugging us before she embraced her aunt. Mary and Josephine were pleased to see their foster mother and went rushing over to tell her about camp. Estelle's caretaker was waiting for her, Ruby's grandmother for her, and the only good-byes left were to the other assistant counselors.

Gerald, of course, went around awkwardly hugging all the girls, and we hugged back. We were a little more enthusiastic with the rest of the guys, and we all traded e-mail addresses.

It was Joe and Craig and Andy who did the major hugging. We'd already said good-bye to

Richard and of course Ross, as well as to Phil and Sue and all the other full counselors, back at camp.

"What's this? 'Muddybiker'?" I said, looking at the screen name Craig gave me.

"Used to be 'NearlyNaked,' but I've grown up," Craig said, and we laughed.

Finally—coming around the far end of the parking lot—was Elizabeth's mom in their Oldsmobile.

"Hi," she called. "I'm the designated driver for the four of you."

Mrs. Price parked a few spaces away from where we were standing and—smiling warily, because she never knows when she's going to set Elizabeth off—she got out and opened the trunk for our bags.

"Hi, Mom!" Elizabeth said, and actually walked over and hugged her. Mrs. Price was so surprised, she dropped the car keys but quickly hugged her back. All I could figure was that after listening to the kids at Camp Overlook describe their home lives, Elizabeth must have decided that she was awfully lucky after all and that what mistakes had been made in the past were forgivable.

Dad was waiting for me when I got in the house, and I gave him a bear hug—two for good measure.

"Sure seems like camp agreed with you, honey," he said, looking me over.

"You mean I'm *fat*?"

"I mean you look like you got plenty of fresh air and exercise."

"I did. I ate everything in sight, but I guess I managed to work it off," I told him. "Any word from Sylvia?"

"Things have settled down a little. At least Nancy's no worse. The antibiotics appear to be working, but her kidneys have shut down and she's on dialysis. Doctors are hoping that after a rest they'll begin functioning again. But it's going to be a long road, I'm afraid."

I couldn't bear the sadness in his voice. "Dad, does this mean that the wedding's postponed indefinitely?"

"No. Sylvia's already decided that once the danger's past, we'll set a date, whether Nancy can be in the wedding or not."

If Nancy didn't show, would that make me maid of honor? I wondered selfishly. What I said was, "Well, that's good news, then. How's Lester?"

"Well, he's been out most of the time, but from the little I've seen of him, he's fine."

I liked coming home to find things going okay. Not perfect, but okay. Up in my room my rubber plant needed watering, but the jungle bedspread

looked inviting, and everything seemed larger than
it had before. There's nothing like a bunk bed in
a primitive cabin to make you appreciate the com-
forts of home.

There was a lot of e-mail waiting for me. I love
to see the little yellow flag pop up on my mailbox,
meaning that someone's thinking about me,
telling me something. There was even a message
from Patrick. I read that one first:

> Don't suppose you can access your e-mail
> from camp, but here's a "Hi" anyhow.
> Taking two summer school courses—
> European history and psychology—they're
> more work than I thought. Let me know
> when you get back.
> **Patrick**

> Figured you'd want to know there are girls
> swarming all over me here in Texas. They
> seem to like a guy who s-s-s-stutters. Wish
> you were here to fend them off.
> (Don't I wish!) Just wish you were here.
> **Eric**

> Saw Patrick at the mall, and he says
> you're at camp already. Nobody tells me
> anything.
> **Jill**

> I called you last night, and your dad said
> you were at Camp Overlook. Sounds like
> something Leslie and I might like to do.
> We were talking about that the other
> day—how our ideal job would be guides
> in national parks. We both like to hike.

Call me when you get back if you want to.
**Lori**

I told Jill you would be at camp. I don't
know why she thinks everyone's in the
loop but her.
**Karen**
P. S. Did you know that Mark and Penny
are going out?

*Whoa!* I thought. Maybe Patrick and Penny really
*were* kaput!

Lester came in about four. He'd been playing
tennis all afternoon and was wet with perspiration,
but I hugged him anyway.

"Careful. You'll smell like eau-de-armpits," he said.

"I don't care. I'm just glad to be home," I told
him. "Everything looks good to me, even you."
Then I remembered. "Listen, Lester," I said, pulling away from him. "It was *you* who blabbed to
Jack Harrigan about the guys swimming naked,
wasn't it?"

Lester faked surprise. *"Moi?"*

"Yes, you! What did you tell him?"

"I did not tell him the guys were naked."

"Well, what *did* you say?"

Lester wiped his face and neck with his towel. "I
merely said that I understood there had been a
shortage of swim trunks the other night and that
I'd be glad to supply some."

"Les-ter!" I bellowed.

"What's this? What's this?" Dad called from the kitchen.

"Nothing," I said, and gave Lester a look.

Dad was making one of my favorite meals, shrimp gumbo, and we could smell it all over the house. It drowned out the smell of Lester's sweaty shirt. "Who were you playing tennis with?" I asked. "Not Eva, was it?" That was one old girlfriend of Lester's I couldn't stand.

"No, there's no woman in my life at the moment," he said.

"Too bad," I said, settling down on the couch with a magazine. "Take lots of cold showers."

"Cold showers? Do I have a disease or something?"

"So you won't keep thinking of sex, Lester."

He laughed. "Cold showers can't keep me from thinking of sex, Al. Acupuncture wouldn't keep me from thinking of sex. Riots, floods, and heavy artillery wouldn't do it. It's carved in a man's brain. There's a little section up there between the right and the left hemispheres that's labeled S-E-X. Besides," he added, "from what I heard, there was a lot going on at camp besides toasting marshmallows."

Dad came in just then with some lemonade for us while we waited for the shrimp gumbo to cook.

"Am I interrupting something?" he asked cautiously.

"No, we're discussing sex," I teased. "Lester thinks there was a lot of it going on up at camp, but he's dead wrong."

"Glad to hear that. Nothing more serious than a little petting, I hope," said Dad, trying to sound enlightened and cool.

"Petting?" I asked. He made it sound like a *zoo!*

"Letting a guy feel you up," Lester translated. Dad sounds so *antiquated* sometimes.

Dad winced. "What has happened to the English language?" he complained. "That sounds so vulgar, Les. Can't you at least say 'fondle'?"

"'Feel' . . . 'fondle' . . . one has one syllable, Dad, and the other has two," Lester said.

Dad smiled a little, shook his head, and went back to the kitchen. It was good to be home. I wanted Dad to stay like he was forever—wonderfully warm and caring and old-fashioned—and Lester to stay hip and funny. Then I wondered if I really knew *what* I wanted. Some things to change, I guess, and others to stay the same. Yet if things stayed the same, Dad would never marry. Pamela's folks would go on fighting. You can't pick and choose, I decided. Life happens, ready or not.

It wasn't till later that evening that I remembered to call Patrick. Does that mean you're over a breakup, I wondered, when you even forget to answer an ex-boyfriend's e-mail?

I dialed his number. "Hi," I said. "I'm back."

"O-*kay*!" he said. "How was it?"

"Hard. Fun. Interesting. Exhausting."

"Sounds so academic."

"We went skinny-dipping," I said.

There was a pause. "I stand corrected," he said. "Just the girls?"

"Guys and girls together."

"Not very academic at all," said Patrick.

"So what's up?" I asked him.

"I wondered if I could get some help on an assignment," he said. "I could come over."

"*You're* asking for *my* help?" I said. "Patrick, I didn't know there was any subject in the world you couldn't handle."

"Surprise!" he said. "In psych we have to do an interview, and I wondered if I could interview you."

"Why?"

"We're doing some kind of statistical thing. Data gathering and statistical correlation."

Patrick's advanced-placement courses always sound so impossible to me. "What do you want to know?" I asked.

"Well, I thought it would be easier if I just came over. That okay?"

"Sure."

"About nine? It would help if you had a baby book or something—a record of childhood illnesses and stuff."

"Yeah, I'll look for it," I said.

"See you," he said.

"Patrick's coming over," I told Dad. "He wants to see my baby book."

"Oh?" said Dad.

"Your *baby* book?" Lester said. "Call him back and tell him there's still time to cancel. Does he know you were born bald?"

I gave Lester a look. "Where is it? My book?" I asked Dad.

"The bottom drawer of my desk," he answered.

It was a white book with pink letters on the silk cover: BABY DEAR. And there, on the very first page—I remembered it now—was the photo of me just a few hours after I was born, my eyes closed, mouth puckered, fists clenched. Lester was right. No hair whatsoever.

I carefully leafed through the book, because some of the photos were pasted in, some were loose. *First Outing,* it said at the top of one page, and there was a picture of Mom in a pretty spring dress, holding me up to the camera, a cotton sunbonnet on my bald head. *Baby's Friends, Baby's Favorite Toys, Health Record, First Birthday . . .*

Stitched to the page describing my third birthday was a lock of fine silky hair, blond with a faint orange tint to it. *We've got another strawberry blonde in the family,* Mom had written below.

A photo of me at Christmas on Dad's lap, a photo of Lester, gingerly handing me a small car . . .

Mom's notes: *Alice Kathleen—a bright happy little soul! . . . Around the age of two, when Alice would discover a parent missing temporarily, she would say, "Where's a mama?" or "Where's a daddy go?" . . . Upon waking from a nap and seeing Lester's shoes on the floor, she asked, "Where did feet go?" . . .*

And further on: *Age three: Was inspecting the beloved but raggedy bear she took to bed every night, which had long since lost its face, and said, "Daddy, we've got to buy this kid a mouth." . . . Alice calls Lester her "bruzzer."*

Then three small pictures of my mother— holding me on a merry-go-round, blowing soap bubbles with me, kissing my forehead. . . . Suddenly that sinking, smothering, sad feeling. It comes on so suddenly that I don't even feel it till it knocks me over, like a wave in the ocean. I gulp, I blink, I catch my breath, and then it's gone. Sometimes it comes again within a week, and sometimes months go by without my feeling it. I told Dad about it once and he said, "It's called longing, Al. It's missing somebody."

# 13

# Viva la Difference

Patrick always seems taller when I haven't seen him for a while. He stood at the door in his tennis shorts and T-shirt, his fair skin freckled, his red hair hanging down one side of his forehead.

I think my heart will always skip a beat for Patrick. They say that's true of your first boyfriend. The big question, of course, was whether his heart still skipped a beat for me. I doubted it. Still, I couldn't help wondering just how far he would have to bend down to kiss me now.

"So, hi," he said. "Welcome back."

"Come on in," I told him. I noticed he had a notebook under his arm.

Dad was stretched out on the couch listening to music, and Lester was in the kitchen. We took over the dining room table, and Dad waved to Patrick, then closed his eyes again. When he's missing Sylvia, he always listens to the music they've enjoyed together.

"You look great," Patrick said to me.

"So do you. What have you been doing, besides school?"

"Teaching tennis."

"Really?"

"Yeah. At day camp. Five afternoons a week. My courses are both in the mornings." He saw my baby book open to the photo of me just after I was born. "Let me see that," he said, and I slid the book toward him. He studied it and grinned. "Didn't have a lot of hair, did you?"

"Bald as a grapefruit," I said.

He went back to his assignment sheet. There was a series of questions about "firsts," and I found the right page in the baby book and read them off to him. First laugh? *Twelve weeks*. First crawl? *Eight months*. First word? *Thirteen months, "ba" for "ball."* First step? . . .

"Why do you need to know all this stuff, Patrick?" I asked.

"It's just an exercise in gathering data. It's not very scientific, and that's probably what we're supposed to learn from this assignment."

"Why not just go through *your* baby book?"

"That would be too subjective."

"Okay. What else do you need to know?"

"Social development," said Patrick. "Did you have any of the following?" He slid a paper toward me. "Just put an 'X' in the appropriate box."

I looked the paper over. "I haven't the foggiest idea!" I turned toward Dad. "Dad," I called, "when I was little, did I suck my thumb, throw temper tantrums, exhibit separation anxiety, or wet the bed?"

Lester stuck his head in from the kitchen. "What's this? Did she wet the bed? Why, she was a first-class, grade-A, government-certified soaker!"

"Lester!" I said, and looked at Dad again.

"Gosh, Al, that's something Marie would have remembered," he said. "If it's not in your baby book, I don't know. You sucked your thumb till you were three, I remember that, and you cried if we left you with a sitter, but as for the rest . . ."

"It's okay," said Patrick. "I'll put down two 'no's' and two 'yes's.'" He looked over the assignment again. "All right, on a scale of one to ten, one being the lowest and ten the highest, how would you rate your abilities in science and math?"

"Two," I said.

"I don't believe it," said Patrick.

"Okay. One," I said.

He smiled, shook his head, and wrote down 2.

"Your abilities in social studies—history, sociology, stuff like that?"

I shrugged. "Seven, maybe?"

"Art?"

"Seven."

"Language arts?"

"Nine and a half," I told him. Patrick wrote down 9.

"I can't understand what you're going to do with all this stuff," I told him after we'd gone through another fifteen minutes of questions.

"We're trying to see if there's any correlation between things that happened to us when we were small and our abilities in high school," said Patrick. "But I talked to a guy who took this course last semester, and he says what it's really going to show is all the things that could make for a false correlation. We learn how to do a study right by doing it wrong."

"Whatever," I said.

Patrick's always so far ahead of me that I'm not sure I know what he's talking about. Maybe he really *is* the kind of guy who should get through four years of high school in three.

"Take it from me," Lester called from the kitchen, "She really *was* a soaker."

"Lester, will you shut up?" I said. "Go out for the evening or something."

"I will. I'm just waiting for a babe to call. If the phone rings, guys, I'll get it," he said, and it sounded like his mouth was full of potato chips.

"Okay, we're almost done," said Patrick. He glanced over at me. "Can I get you anything? Water? Tranquilizers?"

"This is my house, remember?" I said.

"Oh, right!" said Patrick. "This is the last set. On a scale of one to ten, how would you rate your popularity?"

I thought I'd probably check in at about a six or seven, but I wasn't going to tell Patrick that.

"Eight," I said. He wrote it down.

"On a scale of one to ten, how comfortable are you with members of the opposite sex?"

"Ten," I lied.

"How many boys have you kissed in your lifetime, excluding family members?"

"Patrick!" I said.

He didn't even look up. "How many guys did you kiss at Camp Overlook, and on a scale of one to ten, how would you rate them?"

I laughed. "This interview is over. The whole thing was bogus, wasn't it?"

He laughed too and closed his notebook. "No. Cross my heart. Except for the last set, which I sort of sneaked in there. Hey, it's a nice night out. Want to sit on the porch for a little bit?"

"Sure," I said, and we got up and went to the door.

It was a beautiful clear night out, and it reminded me, with a pang, of the night Patrick and I had that fight and broke up. I almost didn't want to sit in the swing with him for fear it would take me back to that place where my world . . . well, my social life, anyway . . . seemed to revolve around Patrick. Before I got involved with the backstage crew of the Drama Club at school. Before I felt as comfortable with myself as I do now.

But then, there was Patrick holding the screen door open for me, so I followed him out and we sat down a few inches apart.

"Been a while since we did this," he said, and smiled at me.

"Yeah, it has," I said, and smiled back. We pushed against the floor with our feet.

"So . . . are you going out with anyone?" he asked.

"Not at the moment."

"Me either. I'm girl-less."

"So I heard."

He shrugged. "I guess school and band and track and tennis are about all I can take on this year."

"So . . . no time for romance, huh?"

"You could say that. Anyway, it was a dumb idea to think you'd like it if I went out with you both. Penny thought so too."

"Chalk one up for Penny," I said dryly, then decided to go for it. "So why *did* you two break up?"

"She was just. . . . Well, Penny's a nice girl, but she was way too demanding of my time, and I can't blame her."

I didn't say anything.

"Besides," Patrick said with a grin in my direction, "she wasn't you."

"Well, of course she's not me," I said.

He leaned sideways and kissed me lightly on the forehead before he stood up. "Viva la difference," he said. "See you later. Thanks for your help, Alice."

*Viva la difference?* Now what did he mean by that, exactly? I've heard Lester say it before when he's talking about the differences between men and women. Talking about a woman's curves, for example.

Did Patrick mean that he was glad Penny and I were different from each other because he liked variety? Was he saying he was glad that I'm me because he found something missing in Penny? He said she was demanding. Good. At least I'd found *something* about her to hate.

The fact was, I wasn't really hurt that Patrick hadn't stayed longer—that he hadn't given me a real kiss. That he hadn't asked me to go with him again. Relieved mostly, I guess. Maybe both of us wanted to see what else—*who* else—was out there. Besides, did I really want a boyfriend who was more interested in getting through high school in three years than he was in me? I don't think so.

"Bye, Patrick," I said to the breeze, and went back inside the house.

Aunt Sally called about ten. Sometimes I think she makes a note on the calendar when it's time to check up on us. I know she promised Mother to look after Lester and me, and since we moved to Maryland, she feels the least she can do is call. How she and Uncle Milt raised Carol, their only daughter, to be the free spirit she is, I don't know, but Dad says that talking to Aunt Sally sets him back forty years.

It was Lester who answered the phone. Les always says as little as possible to Aunt Sally because he hates the way she tries to pry personal information out of him.

"Hi, Sal!" I heard him say. "Things are fine here. How are you?" And then, "Oh, I think she enjoyed camp a lot. She's right here; I'll let you talk to her."

"Thanks," I muttered as I took the phone. Then, "Hi, Aunt Sally."

"Oh, dear, I just wanted to know how things

went at camp. What a wonderful experience for you! The children must have been so grateful!" came her voice.

"Well, I can't say that, exactly, but I did have a good time," I said.

She laughed self-consciously. "But not *too* much fun, I hope."

I didn't answer for a moment. I could have told her about skinny-dipping, I suppose. I do things like that sometimes just to hear her flip out. But Aunt Sally's probably doing the best she can, so I said, "No, it was just right."

"That's good," she said. "I know you're growing up, Alice, and I try to prepare myself for the day you'll be a young woman, but I never know quite what to ask. I try to think what Marie would have wanted me to tell you, but I'm just not very good at this. I'm afraid Carol had to raise herself in the sex department."

I envisioned a store with a sex department between housewares and shoes.

"You're doing fine," I told her. We talked then about Sylvia and the wedding being postponed, about how Uncle Milt and Carol were doing, how Carol had just mailed off a box of clothes she thought I might like, and how I was going to spend the rest of my summer. I think this was the closest to a real conversation Aunt Sally and I had ever had. I decided that from now on, now that I was "growing up," I would try to be a little more understanding of Aunt Sally.

After I hung up, I checked my e-mail one more time. There was a message from Gerald:

> Hi, Alice. Just want to apologize for what happened at camp. I knew I came on too strong. I tend to do that. Scare girls away, I guess. Anyway, I wanted you to know that I'm taking your advice and going to audition as a reader for Books for the Blind. I'll see how well I do and if they think I'm any good, maybe I'll major in broadcast journalism. Thanks for the support. Take care.
> G. E.

Dad insists that I get a checkup at the dentist's and doctor's every summer. Most of my friends see a doctor only when they're sick. But Dad says it gives him peace of mind, so I go. This year, to get it over with, I scheduled them both for the same day.

I went to the dentist first.

"You know, Alice," he said, "last time you were here, I said you have a little bite problem—the way your teeth come together in front. You might want to see an orthodontist about it. I can recommend someone if you like."

He *had* mentioned it, but in such an offhand

way that I had put it out of my mind. I felt my shoulders sag. "You mean braces, don't you?"

"Probably, but I don't think it's a serious problem. I've seen a whole lot worse."

"Well, I'm not doing anything till after my dad's wedding," I said. "I don't want to be wearing braces then."

"Fair enough," the dentist said. "When's the wedding?"

"This fall sometime," I told him, and made up my mind I wouldn't even *think* about braces until the wedding was over.

But I was thinking about them anyway—how much I'd hate them—when I signed in at Dr. Beverly's later. Once inside the narrow hallway, though, I knew the routine. The nurse weighed me and measured my height, then gave me a paper cup with my last name on it and told me to go in the rest room and leave a urine specimen in the cup.

It's sort of weird, you know? You're supposed to urinate a little in the toilet, then hold the cup under you and pee into that till it's about half full—you don't want it running over and dripping all over the place—and then pee the rest in the toilet. When you're all through, you open the tiny cupboard door in the wall and set your cup on a shelf lined with a paper towel. On the other side of the wall is another tiny door leading to the doctor's laboratory. A technician on the other side opens the other door every so often, takes out any cups that are there, and does an analysis of the urine—like living in a nunnery or something, where you can communicate with people only through a hole in the wall.

I flushed the toilet. Then, carefully holding my half-filled cup, I leaned over and opened the cupboard door. At that very moment the door on the other side opened, and I found myself looking smack into the face of a fortyish woman with glasses and a mole on her cheek.

Good grief! What was I supposed to do? What was I supposed to say?

"Hi," she said.

I was so flustered, I set down my cup and quickly banged the door shut.

Instantly I felt my face flush. Now why had I done *that?* It just seemed so personal somehow, like I wasn't supposed to be looking at her. But *she* wasn't the one with her underpants down to her ankles! *Why* couldn't I have said something funny like, *We've got to stop meeting like this!* When would I quit doing such stupid, embarrassing things? But I already knew the answer to that. Never, ever, ever.

# 14

# The Big Announcement

"So how are you?" Dad asked at dinner. "Everything okay?"

Lester always cringes when Dad asks that, because I used to embarrass him hugely. I'd always have something to tell about what went on at the doctor's office because . . . well, who else was there to tell? Family, I mean.

Elizabeth and Pamela are shocked that I can talk to my dad and brother about the things I do, even though Lester says he doesn't want to hear it, which I don't believe for one moment. I guess it's because I don't have a mother. I started out asking Dad and Lester questions when I was too young to be embarrassed, and once I got started, it just seemed natural to keep on asking.

But by the time I got home, I'd recovered from my embarrassment. Besides, I was getting a stepmom, and I couldn't wait till Sylvia and I were having *intimate* conversations. Just the two of us. So when Dad asked how things went with my doctors' appointments, I replied, "Fine. No problems." I decided not to even mention braces for now. Dad didn't need this to deal with too.

"Whew!" said Lester. "That's good to hear."

"It certainly is," said Dad.

"No puddles on the examining table? No gagging when he examined your throat?" Lester asked.

"Nope," I said. "I'm good for another year."

"Well, *I've* got news, then," said Lester.

"Oh?" said Dad, suddenly focusing on Lester.

"I got an offer I can't refuse," said Lester.

"Not from a woman, I hope," said Dad.

"No, and I think even you will agree to this, Dad. The last time I talked about finding a place of my own, you said to at least wait for a while after Sylvia moves in so she won't feel like she's breaking up the family, remember?"

"Yes . . . ," Dad said warily.

"Well, I was playing tennis with Paul Sorenson this morning, and he says that a friend of his father's—an old-timer named Otto Watts—needs someone to live in the second floor of his house. He's got one of these big Victorian houses in Takoma Park near the D.C. line. They made the upstairs into an apartment for their younger daughter when she was in college, but she's out on her own now, and Mrs. Watts is dead. His children think he ought to be in a retirement home, but he won't hear of it. So here's the deal: Because he knows Paul's father, Mr. Watts is offering the apartment to Paul if he'll get two other guys to share it, with the understanding that one of us will be there evenings all the time in case Mr. Watts needs us. He has an aide come in during the day. We'd have to do all the light maintenance around the place—mow the grass, paint, trim the bushes, that kind of stuff—and pay for our utilities. But other than that, it's rent-free. George Palamas is going to move in with Paul, and they asked if I wanted to be the third."

I sat as still as the baked potato on my plate. I was too stunned to even think whether this was good news or bad news. Dad looked surprised too. Lester leaving?

"I know Paul. Do I know George?" Dad asked.

"He's been here, but you may not remember him. He's responsible. Works for an insurance company."

"Well, it certainly does seem like a good deal, Lester. But what about visitors? What about noise? Is he going to complain if you play your CDs or have late parties?"

"He's deaf," said Lester. "But he's sharp as a tack. Funny, too. Paul asked him if we could have friends in, if the noise would bother him, and he said he'd just remove his hearing aid."

Dad smiled. "Do you think you can keep the promise that one of you three will be there every evening?" Dad asked.

"That'll be the hardest part, but for a rent-free place, we're willing to do it. If it were just two of us and we could never go anywhere together, I don't think so. Besides, anytime Mr. Watts's family takes him somewhere—out for the evening or on vacation—we can all be out too. It's not like we're prisoners forever."

Dad toyed with his veal chop. "You've talked of moving closer to campus, though."

"I know, but I'd never get as sweet a deal as this one, Dad. I really want to try it, and now that the wedding's postponed, I think I ought to move out, give you and Sylvia some privacy."

I kept looking from Dad to Lester, Lester to Dad. Just because Dad was marrying Sylvia, did *every*-thing have to change? I suddenly wanted to retract everything I'd said about wanting something to happen this summer. Was *I* going to have to move out too to give them privacy? How much privacy did they need? They could always close their door. Then I realized that Lester's room is right next to theirs. Maybe that *would* be a little awkward.

"Well, it certainly seems like a good opportunity," Dad said at last. "Paul is in school too; it's a lucky break for you both."

Lester beamed and looked at me. How could I say it was okay with me? Lester had lived with us my entire life. I'd be lost without him! I could see me eating breakfast alone on Saturday mornings. Making dinner by myself when it was our night to cook. Standing at the doorway of Lester's empty room when everyone else had gone to bed and I had a worry that only Lester could understand. I hated the tremor in my voice when I asked, "Will I be able to visit you?"

"Sure!" Lester said. "It's only a couple of miles from here. We'll have you to dinner! You can drop by on weekends."

My mind suddenly did a turnaround and started racing in the other direction. I could see me eating lunch on Sundays in my brother's apartment with two other handsome guys. I could see making spaghetti sauce for them when they had a party. I could see me driving over there after I got my license and sitting on the front porch on summer nights and being introduced to Lester's friends.

"Well, I think it's a wonderful idea too!" I said. "I think it's time that Lester had a place of his own."

Both Dad and Lester looked surprised, like they'd expected a protest.

"Well, then, I'll tell Paul I'm in," said Lester.

"When will you be moving out?" asked Dad.

"Mr. Watts is having the place painted, so it won't be ready till the middle of September, but he says there's no reason we can't move some of our stuff in if we keep it in the middle of the floor."

I imagined Lester and Paul and George inviting Pamela and Elizabeth and me to dinner. I imagined George and Paul and Lester going to the movies and inviting me and Elizabeth and Pamela to come along. I imagined Paul and Lester and George going shopping at Safeway to stock their refrigerator and Elizabeth and me and Pamela going along to help. I imagined . . .

"So what's going through *your* mind?" Les said to me. "Planning to take over my room the minute I move out?"

"No," I said brightly. "Just thinking about the future, that's all."

It was the first thing I wanted to talk about when our gang met the next Sunday at Mark Stedmeister's pool. It was hard to find a time we could all get together at once, because most of us had part-time jobs. I was working days at the Melody Inn; Elizabeth was baby-sitting her little brother; and Pamela was working part-time for a dog-walking service.

The biggest change I'd noticed in our group was that we sat around and talked more. The guys weren't constantly trying to push each other in the pool, or seeing who could make the biggest cannonball and splash everyone on the deck.

In junior high our conversations were mostly the boys joking about something and the girls laughing. Joke . . . laugh . . . joke . . . laugh. Now we were actually having real conversations. I was impressed at how adult we sounded.

"Big news. Lester's moving out," I said as we lounged about on the deck, our bodies covered with sunblock.

Pamela and Elizabeth stared at me. "Oh, Al-ice!" they wailed in unison.

"Aren't you sad?" asked Elizabeth.

I began to wonder if this really was a tragedy and I just didn't know it yet.

"Well, he's only a couple of miles away, and he's sharing an apartment with two cute guys," I said, stretching it a bit, since I didn't know either Paul Sorenson or George Palamas.

I could see the wheels turning in Pamela's head. "Could we see his apartment?" she asked.

"Oh, sure! Lester said we could visit anytime." Now I was stretching the truth so far, I could almost hear it snap.

Elizabeth was all enthusiasm. "Oh, Alice, we could help them decorate! We could go over on moving day and cook for them and everything!" she said.

"We could have a housewarming party for them. In their apartment!" said Pamela. "Oh, man, this is *major*!"

"Maybe they'd let us have the apartment some night for our own party," said Brian. "Now that would be cool."

"Sweeeeet!" agreed Mark.

I began to feel as though Lester's apartment was getting a lot more publicity than he would have liked.

"When's moving day?" Pamela asked.

I knew I had to back off. "I'm not sure," I said. "I'll let you know." And I was relieved when the conversation turned to other things.

"Anyone seen Patrick lately?" Justin asked. "I thought his courses would be over by now." Justin was sitting by Elizabeth. One minute it looked like they might be getting chummy again, the next minute Jill was in his lap.

"Patrick came by the other night," I said, waving off a fly.

Everyone looked at me.

"He was doing a psych assignment," I explained, "and needed to interview someone."

"Can you imagine Patrick asking anyone for help?" said Karen.

"I can't," said Penny. "Patrick Long is the most self-sufficient person I know."

Somehow I resented her answering, even though Karen had asked a question. I guess I'd wanted her to sound surprised—hurt, even—that he'd come by to see me, now that they'd broken up. I ignored her.

"What's this I hear about Gwen and Legs splitting up?" Mark asked. "Leo says he drove up to see her at that camp and she was making out with some guy there."

Pamela and Elizabeth and I broke into laughter, remembering that movie-star kiss. "Yeah, sure. She was making out, all right," I said. "And Legs couldn't be happier that he can go out now with the girl he's been two-timing Gwen with in the first place."

Mark hadn't known that we knew about Legs's new girlfriend. The conversation got general then—who was going with whom, what everybody had been doing over the summer.

Patrick came just as we were taking orders for calzones. Take-out Taxi will deliver.

"My man!" Brian said when he saw Patrick, and they punched each other on the shoulder. Guys have such *stupid* greetings!

"How you doing?" Patrick asked, looking around the whole group. His smile extended to me. I was mainly watching Penny, though. She just turned her head away from him. It was then I noticed that she and Mark were playing footsie. Things sure do change. It hadn't seemed so long ago that Mark and Pamela were going out, but then Mark dumped potato salad down the back of Pamela's bikini bottom, and it was good-bye, Mark!

I was tired of baking in the sun, so I got up and jumped in the pool. Elizabeth and Patrick jumped in too.

"How did you do on the psych interview?" I asked Patrick.

"Got an A minus," said Patrick.

"Why the minus?"

"Because I should have asked a few more questions."

"What kind of an interview was it?" asked Elizabeth.

"I had to interview someone about childhood experiences so we could see if there was any connection between what had gone on in childhood and what was going on now."

"Sounds interesting," said Elizabeth.

Patrick grinned. "She was an interesting girl."

"So was there any correlation?" I asked.

"That's what we're working on this week, when we pool our results. It's not a valid study."

"I'm grateful for that," I said. "I'd hate to have you know something about me that I didn't know."

I wasn't paying as much attention to Patrick right then, though, as I was to Pamela. She was sitting around with the others, but it looked as though her mind was a thousand miles away. I realized what I'd been missing this summer; the old, outrageous, fast-track Pamela, who always seemed a step or two ahead of the rest of us. Even at camp she'd seemed to take a backseat in whatever we did; and watching her now—her knees pulled up to her chest, her eyes on a tree—I vowed to give her more time and attention before school started.

"Okay," she said the next day when I called her, just to talk. "I got the whole story." I could hear a new CD by the Velvet Pistols playing in the background.

"Of what?" I asked.

"Of what happened between Patrick and Penny."

"Who did you get it from? Patrick or Penny?"

"Karen."

"Oh, come *on*, Pamela! You can't believe half of

what Karen tells you. If she doesn't have any good gossip, she'll make it up."

"She got it straight from Penny."

"I'll bet."

"Well, do you want to hear it or not?"

Of course I did.

"Penny just felt that she came second in Patrick's life."

"Second to what?"

"I'm not sure, but that's what she told Karen. His courses, maybe. Probably you."

"Don't be ridiculous."

"She said that a couple of times Patrick even made the mistake of calling her "Alice.""

I had to smile. "I can imagine how Penny took to *that*!"

"Well, it wasn't just that. She also said that a lot of the time she didn't think he was all there."

"Now what did she mean by that? Patrick's one of the brightest guys I know!"

"She meant that he wasn't all that focused on her. He had his mind on other things."

"That's Patrick," I said. "But I can't imagine why she'd suspected I was in the picture again. Except for that e-mail message from Patrick, we hadn't seen or spoken to each other since school let out."

"That's not what Penny thinks."

"So why doesn't she ask *me*?"

"Oh, come on. She wouldn't humiliate herself like that. Admit it, now. Doesn't it give you even the slightest satisfaction to know that *she's* jealous of *you*?"

"Yes," I said, laughing.

"And isn't there just the teeniest, tiniest bit of satisfaction in knowing that after she took him away from you, he was the one who lost interest?"

"Yep," I told her.

"You and Patrick ought to go out sometime right under her nose, just to get even."

"Oh, I don't know," I said.

"I don't understand you, Alice. It's not a sin to want to rub it in a little."

"Maybe I like my new freedom," I told her.

In the background, the lead singer for the Velvet Pistols was shouting out the words. I'm not even sure you could call it singing:

"I wanna make you,
I wanna break you,
Baby, you're mine tonight."

And then the band, all the guys together, started moaning a sort of syncopated "*Uh*-huh, *Uh*-huh, *Uh*-huh," which was supposed to sound like they were having sex, I guess.

Finally, Pamela said, "I'm really down, Alice.

Everyone else has a job with *people* for the rest of the summer. All I've got for company are dogs. Find out exactly when Lester's moving, will you? I want at least one thing to look forward to."

# 15

# The Go-Between

Dad seemed to need me more around the house once I was back. I'm not sure what it was, but it was as though he'd lost his bearings after Sylvia postponed the wedding. I guess I'd call him distracted, but not quite coming apart at the seams. Maybe everyone has a limited amount of patience, I thought, and he had about used his up.

I mentioned this at the Melody Inn.

"His mind is on Sylvia, that's the problem," I said to Marilyn Rawley, after we had unpacked some boxes UPS had delivered. Marilyn is one of Lester's old girlfriends, who works for Dad as his assistant manager.

"I've noticed," Marilyn said, scooping up her long brown hair in back and planting it firmly on top of her head with a wide comb. "I had to remind him last week that our paychecks were due. The music instructors hadn't been paid."

But I was staring at her hand. I reached up and took hold of her ring finger. There was a small oval diamond set in white gold.

"Marilyn?" I said, studying her face, and she broke into a wide smile. "That guy you've been going out with? Jack?"

She nodded.

I didn't know whether to smile or cry. I had *so* wanted Lester to marry Marilyn! More than any of the other girls he ever dated—Crystal Harkins, even—I'd wanted it to be Marilyn.

She understood, because she put a finger to my lips and said, "Don't say it."

I swallowed, then managed to congratulate her. "Have you told Dad?" I asked.

"No. Jack just proposed last night."

"Oh, Marilyn, Jack is so lucky! I hope he knows how lucky he is, and I hope you'll be deliriously happy every day for the rest of your life!" I burbled.

She hugged me and laughed. "Nobody is happy every day of her life, Alice. But when he asked me, I just knew he was the right one."

I spent the rest of the afternoon straightening the merchandise in the Gift Shoppe and wrapping purchases and making change and wondering how you knew when you'd met the "right one." How soon had Dad known that about Sylvia? A lot sooner, I guess, than Sylvia knew that about Dad.

Gwen had even thought for a while that Legs was "the one" for her. Just how wrong can you be?

"Your shirts aren't back from the laundry yet because you didn't send them out," I told Dad one evening. "Your laundry bag is still in your closet. Want me to take them in for you?"

He looked exasperated. He also kept forgetting to pick up milk and bananas—the things we use up faster than anything else—so I'd begun checking the refrigerator regularly and walking to the 7-Eleven to get them when I saw we were running low. Checking his shirts. He had worked so hard to get the house ready for Sylvia, and who knew when she'd come back?

After dinner he went out to putter around in the garden, pulling weeds, spreading a little mulch, watering. Then he went up to his room, and I saw him sitting at his desk when I walked by.

Later, when Les and I were cleaning up the kitchen, Sylvia called.

"Dad's up in his room writing a letter to you," I said. "I'll get him."

"Well, let me talk to you first, Alice. How *are* you? I don't think we've talked since you went to camp." Her voice was as lilting as ever.

"Oh, I'm fine. I had a really good time, but I like being home for the rest of the summer."

"I know how you feel. I wish *I* could be home. How's Ben holding up? Really."

"He's missing you," I said.

"Oh, I know. And I'm missing him terribly."

"How's Nancy?"

"Better. Her kidneys are starting to function again. She still needs dialysis, but not as often. We're hopeful."

"Will you . . . will you be back before Christmas?" I asked plaintively.

"Oh, definitely," she said. "But I don't want to get Ben's hopes up that I'm coming back too much sooner until we know for sure. How are *you* doing, Alice?"

"I'm marking time," I told her.

"How?"

"Everything's on hold."

"The wedding, you mean."

"Yes." I swallowed. "I looked at the calendar this morning and . . ."

"I know," she finished for me. "The day we were supposed to be married. I've been feeling sad all day."

"Me too. But the one exciting thing that's happening is that Lester's moving out," I told her. "Well, exciting and sad both, I guess."

"What?"

"It's a really good deal. He gets the apartment

rent-free. I'll let Dad tell you all about it, but Lester said I could visit whenever I wanted." Somehow it seemed that the more people I talked to about Lester's moving, the more generous I made Lester sound. "I just wish you were here, though, to take care of Dad, Sylvia. Then I'd have one less person to worry about."

"Why? Alice, what's wrong?"

"He's sad. He's forgetful. He forgets to take his shirts to the laundry, to stop at the store, to pay all the bills. All he does is mope around and work in the garden."

"You'd better get him to the phone, Alice. I think your dad needs to hear some sweet talk about now."

I grinned. "Okay."

I started upstairs to get Dad just as he was on his way down to refill his coffee cup.

"It's Sylvia, Dad," I said.

His face lit up like Christmas. "Sylvia?" He lunged for the phone, pulled out the telephone stool, and sat down, his back against the wall. His face broke into a hundred little smiling crinkles.

"Sweetheart," he said, adjusting the phone to his ear, and in that moment I heard her say, "Hi, you old, forgetful honey bear. . . ." And I knew it was time for me to clear out.

I went upstairs to sort through my things for the

laundry and saw the glow of Dad's lamp coming from his room. I walked to the doorway. There were his reading glasses on the desk beside a pen and paper. As much as I knew I shouldn't, I tiptoed over to his chair. *I told Sylvia he was writing to her,* I said to myself. *All I'm going to do is take a quick peek and make sure I'd told the truth.*

He must have started the letter on the other side of the page, because the first line was a continuation of something else. But then I read:

> Sylvia, darling, do you know this poem? It's all I can think about these days. sixteenth century, I think:

> O western wind, when wilt thou blow
> That the small rain down can rain?
> Christ, that my love were in my arms
> And I in my bed again!

I swallowed and tiptoed out of the room. Never mind the first two lines. I wasn't even sure what they meant. But the last two! There was something about that poem so urgent, so intense. I could almost feel the longing rise up from the paper. How different it seemed from that Velvet Pistols song: "I wanna make you, I wanna break you. . . ."

If anyone deserved to be deliriously happy for the rest of their lives, it was Dad and Sylvia.

I was at Pamela's house the following week when something happened. Both Elizabeth and I were there. We were lying on Pamela's bed, actually, looking through a magazine, when we heard the doorbell ring and Mr. Jones's footsteps crossing the hall.

"Is it for me, Dad?" Pamela called, and we waited.

Then, almost seconds after we heard the front door open, we heard it close again, hard, with a bang. There was a loud knocking, and then somebody obviously was leaning against the doorbell. *Dingdong-dingdong-dingdong-dingdong.* . . .

"Dad?" Pamela called, and we all sat up, listening.

We heard the door open again, a muffled angry exclamation from Mr. Jones, and then a woman's voice saying, ". . . just to talk. Please!"

*Bang!* went the door again.

"Mom!" gasped Pamela.

"Oh no!" said Elizabeth.

*Dingdong-dingdong-dingdong-dingdong* . . .

"Do you want us to leave?" Elizabeth asked Pamela. "We could go out the back."

"No! I don't want to be here alone with those lunatics!" Pamela said, grabbing hold of us. "He could at least talk to her."

At that moment the doorbell did stop ringing.

"Did you know she was in town?" Elizabeth asked.

"I knew she wanted to come, but I didn't know when." Pamela absently flipped a few more pages of the magazine, but she wasn't looking at them and neither were we.

All at once something hit our window. Pamela rolled off the bed so fast, she kicked me in the leg and pulled us down with her. On the way down she grabbed at the light switch, and the light went out.

"Don't even breathe," said Pamela.

We sat on the floor, our backs against the bed. Another piece of gravel hit the window.

"Pamela," her mom called from outside.

Downstairs the front door opened again, and we heard Mr. Jones say in a low voice, "If you don't leave, I'm calling the police."

"Go ahead. We're not divorced, remember. You can't keep me out of our house," Mrs. Jones yelled at him.

"Dad," Pamela shouted as he shut the door again. "Don't you dare call the police. At least *talk* to her! Maybe then she'll go."

"In a pig's eye," said her father.

But there was no more gravel at the window. No more calling.

"Do you think she's gone?" I whispered.

"Heck no," said Pamela.

Ten minutes went by, though, and nothing happened. But Pamela wouldn't turn on the light. Her dad went back to the TV.

"Man, I wish she'd stayed in Colorado," Pamela said.

"But maybe . . . if she's really sorry for walking out on you . . . he could just give her one more chance?" said Elizabeth.

"How can he give her one more chance if he hates her?" Pamela asked. "She humiliated him. I don't think he'll ever forgive her."

"That's a sin," said Elizabeth.

The phone rang.

"Gwen said she'd call," Pamela told us. "I'll get it," she called to her dad, and picked up the extension in her room. It was Karen.

"Are you ready for this? Big news," we heard her say. *What else can happen tonight?* I was thinking.

Pamela held the phone out so we could all hear even better. "Okay, what?" she asked.

"Guess who's sleeping together."

We looked at each other.

"Sam and Jennifer?" said Pamela.

"They broke up," said Karen.

"They did?" Pamela said, giving me a surprised look, because Sam used to like me.

"Just after school let out," said Karen. "But I'm talking about someone else."

"Who, then?" asked Pamela. "Elizabeth and Alice are here. Tell us."

"Good! Then I won't have to call them. Guess again."

"Penny and Mark?" Elizabeth guessed.

"Not that I know of. I mean, I don't go around *asking,* for Pete's sake!" said Karen.

"No, she just goes around telling," I whispered, but that didn't stop me from listening.

"We give up," said Pamela.

"Jill and Justin."

"Justin?" said Elizabeth. Justin used to like *her.*

"Uh-oh. Have I put my foot in my mouth?" Karen asked. "Liz? You don't still like him, do you?"

"How do you know this, Karen?" I asked, taking the phone.

"Jill told me."

"Well, thanks for that little piece of information," Pamela said.

"And you know who else?" said Karen.

"Karen!" Elizabeth and I said together. At the same time, however, Pamela said, "Who?"

But Karen said, "Well, if you don't want to know . . ." and hung up.

The phone rang again almost immediately.

Pamela picked it up again. "Okay, *who*?" she said.

There was a pause. And then we heard Mrs. Jones's voice saying, "Pamela, *please* make him talk to me."

Elizabeth looked around as though she wanted to find the escape hatch.

"Mom, he doesn't want to! How can I make him?" Pamela said. She wouldn't put the phone against her ear, as though it were so hot it might burn her.

"The last two years have been a nightmare," we heard Mrs. Jones say. "That was the worst mistake I ever made in my life, and I just want to tell him."

I wished Pamela wouldn't let us hear. I felt as though I should cover my ears or go in the bathroom or something.

"You already told him that. You wrote him a letter, remember?" Pamela said. "But he says it's over, Mom. It's just over."

"Well, forget my coming back. All I want is to talk to him."

"If that's your mother, hang up," Pamela's dad yelled from below.

"Dad wants me to hang up," Pamela said into the phone. She sounded like she was going to cry.

"You can't do this to me, Pamela. Please don't hang up!"

"Mom . . . !"

"Pamela!" her Dad yelled again.

Pamela slowly lowered the phone and placed it back in the cradle.

"I don't think we should stay," Elizabeth said. "Do you guys want to come over to my place?"

"I'm afraid of what's going to happen if I leave, but I'm afraid of what will happen if I stay," said Pamela. There were tears in her eyes. "Well, if she's calling from a phone, she must have gone somewhere. We might as well turn on the light."

"Maybe she's calling from a cell phone," I said.

Pamela turned on the light and pulled down her shade. "I absolutely refuse to get caught in the middle!" she declared angrily. "They aren't going to make me their go-between! No *way*!"

"Maybe you could call up that nurse your dad's been dating. Maybe if your mom saw another woman in the house, she'd go away," said Elizabeth, desperate to be helpful.

"*Not* a good idea," said Pamela. She flopped down on the bed again and lay with her arms up over her head. All at once she raised her head and said, "Do you hear footsteps?"

We listened. There were footsteps, all right. The floor creaked, and the next thing we knew, Mrs. Jones was coming through the doorway of Pamela's room, one finger to her lips. Elizabeth and I positively froze.

Pamela's petite, blond mom was wearing jeans and a red polo shirt. She looked good, but her face was a lot more worn than I'd remembered it.

"Oh!" she said, staring at Elizabeth and me. "I didn't know your friends were here."

"Now, Mom," Pamela began, sitting up.

"If you just give the word, Pamela, I'll walk out of your life right now, and you won't ever have to talk to me again."

"I didn't say that, Mom. How did you get in?"

"There's a back door, you know, and I still have a key." Mrs. Jones glanced at Elizabeth and me again, as if asking us to go, but Pamela's fingers were digging into our arms. For Pamela, we stayed put.

Suddenly we heard Mr. Jones's rapid footsteps on the stairs.

"Pamela," he called outside her door. "Is your mother in there?"

Mrs. Jones lunged for the door to lock it, but before she could, it flew open.

"Get the hell out!" Mr. Jones yelled at his wife.

"Are you going to throw me out of our own house, Bill?" Mrs. Jones said.

I wished I could crawl under the bed. I wished I could pull Pamela with me. She always sounds so fast and sassy, but right then she looked like a little girl of seven. Her bottom lip trembled and her eyes were gleaming with tears. I just wanted to hold her.

Mr. Jones reached in and grabbed his wife by the wrist. Mrs. Jones screamed, and he yanked her out of the room. She stumbled against the wall.

And then, while Elizabeth and I watched, heartsick, Pamela sank down on the floor beside her bed, her arms around her legs, face on her knees, and sobbed.

Mrs. Jones turned around and Mr. Jones stopped yelling. And in that silence, Pamela's dad went down the hall to his own bedroom and shut the door.

Pamela's mom stood where she was in the hallway, one hand to her throat. "Oh, my God, Pamela. I'm so sorry, sweetie. I'm just so sorry for all that I've done," she said.

Pamela continued to cry. Elizabeth and I continued to stare.

"Pamela, is there anything I can do?" her mother said, coming back into the room. "What do you really want me to do, sweetheart? Just tell me. Go or stay?"

How could they *do* that to her? I wondered. How could parents make a fifteen-year-old girl decide what they should or shouldn't do?

"Mom," said Pamela, and her nose sounded clogged, "will you just go?"

There was silence.

"Are you sure that's what you want?" her mom asked finally.

I cringed.

"Yes," Pamela said at last.

"Sure?" her mother repeated, taking a step closer. "*Talk* to me, Pamela!"

And suddenly Pamela screamed, "Mom, I'm not *ready* to talk yet! You can't just run off with a guy for almost two years and then expect to come home like nothing's happened."

"Pamela, I didn't exactly run off. I tried to explain it to you then, and I suppose I'm doing an even worse job of explaining now. I've said it was a mistake, and I want to make it up to you. . . ."

"How can you make up for two years of not being here?" Pamela cried. "What could you ever do to 'make it up,' Mom? And right now I just don't want to talk about it because it's all too painful!" She started to cry again. "Yes! Go! Just go!" And she turned the other way.

Mrs. Jones waited a moment longer. Then she went back downstairs, left the house, and shut the door after her. Elizabeth and I sat down on the floor with Pamela between us and let her cry. There wasn't a thing to say, really. Just things to cry.

"Do you think you and your dad might want to

talk later?" I asked. "We could go home now, Pamela, if you want."

"What I want is for you guys to stay right here the rest of the night. You're the two best friends I've ever had," Pamela wept.

So we did.

I was afraid the next morning we'd hear on the news that a woman's body had been found in the Potomac. But two days later Pamela told us her mother had called and said she'd taken an apartment in Wheaton. It looked as though Pamela was going to be the go-between whether she wanted to or not.

I sat in Lester's room the following night while he trimmed his toenails. Lester has very thick toenails, and when a clipping flies across the room, you can hear it land.

"Do you *mind*, Al?" he said. "This is rather personal, you know."

I ignored him because I needed to talk to someone about Pamela. At least he listened while I described what happened.

"I have a theory," I said finally, "that life throws you something awful every five years. When I was five, Mom died. When I was ten, you broke your leg. Now I'm fifteen, and see what's happened to Pamela? What's going to happen when I'm twenty?"

Lester sent another clipping skimming across the floor. "That's about the stupidest thing I ever heard," he said.

"Why?"

"Because it was *me* who broke his leg, not you. And it's Pamela who's got the mother problem."

"But when I think of all the scary, awful things that *could* happen, like Sylvia's plane going down on her way home to marry Dad or—"

"Stuff it, Al! You're ignoring all the good things that happen. Name something nice that's happened recently."

I thought for a moment. "Sylvia calls Dad every day."

"Yep."

"Pamela's mother didn't jump in the river."

"Uh . . . okay. . . ."

"Elizabeth and Ross didn't have sex."

"For Pete's sake, Alice!" Lester said.

I curled up on his bed and watched him finish his clipping. "Lester, here's something I've wondered about. Before the wedding does a bride have to clip her toenails and clean out her navel and scrub every square inch of her body?"

"If she thinks she has lice, I suppose she should."

"I'm serious. I just want to know the etiquette. Are you supposed to present yourself to your new husband all clean and fresh and trimmed and filed and—"

"I don't know. I'm not a woman."

"How much will *you* clean on your wedding day?"

"I suppose I'll take a shower. Give my armpits the old sniff test and see if I really need one." He grinned at me.

I thought some more about weddings. "What if a woman starts her period just before her wedding day?"

I heard Lester let out his breath. "Man, do I ever wish you had a mother," he murmured.

"I need to *know* these things, Lester."

"Do you need to know right now?"

"No, but I'd like to."

"Okay. So what if she does?"

"Well, does she postpone the wedding or what?"

"Al, that's *life!* If her husband can't handle a little thing like that, he shouldn't be getting married at all. Where did you get the idea you have to be perfect? Perfectly scrubbed and manicured and deodorized?"

"The brides all look like that in magazines."

"Magazines aren't life, Al. *I'm* life. *You're* life."

"Yeah, and Pamela's life too, but look how lousy it is." I sat up, my chin on my knees. "You know what, Lester? You know what would give Pamela a really, really big boost?"

"Yeah? What?"

"You could ask her out."

Lester stopped clipping and stared at me, his mouth half open. "You're out of your tree."

"I don't mean in a romantic way. Just take her out for a fun evening and cheer her up."

"Al, I wouldn't take Pamela out if every other girl in the state of Maryland was certifiably insane."

"Why? She adores you, Lester! It would really give her a lift. She's had a crush on you ever since she met you."

"That's exactly why I couldn't take her out, not to mention that I'm seven years older than she is."

"Party pooper," I said with a pout. "Here's a chance for you to do something kind and wonderful for someone who's really hurting."

Lester sighed. "Okay, how's this? I won't ask Pamela out, but you could invite her and Elizabeth over some afternoon to help me pack, and I'll bring in some pizza. You could help me sort through some of my stuff."

"Really, Lester?" I thought of Elizabeth and Pamela and I going through all the secrets in Lester's closet. "That's even better than taking her out! Thank you!" I cried.

"And you know what you can do for me?"

"What?"

"Crawl around the floor and pick up all my nail clippings so I don't walk on them in my bare feet."

I gave him a little smile. "Uh-uh, Lester. That's life!"

# 16

# Confession

Two weeks before school started, a box of clothes arrived from Carol. I love Carol! Every so often she goes through her closet and sends me stuff she doesn't wear anymore. She doesn't send stuff with worn elastic or missing buttons or food stains on them either. Or styles so old that you wouldn't even wear them out on your front porch.

There was a lot to do in those last weeks of August, and e-mails were flying like crazy. Jill wanted to know what everyone was going to wear on the first day of school; Elizabeth thought we ought to take the table nearest the yogurt bar in the cafeteria for lunch; Karen asked if I knew whether she still had to take P. E. if she took diving lessons over the summer. But at the end of her message she wrote, *So do you want to know who else slept together or not?*

The Noble Alice in me would have replied, *Not*

*interested.* But of course that was a lie, so the Truthful Alice typed, *Who?* Karen must not have been online at the time because there was no answer, so I went back to my closet to find a T-shirt to wear the first day—the one with dolphins and sparkles all over it. I held it up in front of me at the mirror and then, on impulse, smiled a toothy smile at myself and wondered how I'd look in braces—if I had sparkles on my teeth as well as my shirt.

I put dividers in my notebook and looked for a pen refill and stuck some tampons in the zip pocket of my backpack. When I went to my computer later, I'd been signed off and had to log on again. There was only one message this time. It was from Karen. I clicked READ.

The message had only ten words:

*Gwen and Legs. Legs told Mark and Mark told me.*

*What?* I thought. *She's crazy!* Gwen wasn't going with Legs anymore, and even if she was, she wouldn't do that. Karen was such a gossip.

I decided to have some friends over while we were still homework-free, so on Saturday I invited Elizabeth and Pamela and Gwen to sleep over. Dad brought up two cots for Pamela and Gwen, and Elizabeth said she'd sleep in my double bed with me.

"Hey! Camp!" Gwen said when she saw the cots. We laughed.

"I am so wired!" said Elizabeth, flopping down on my bed and dropping her bag on the floor. "I've got three subjects I hate this year: American politics, geometry, and biology."

"What did you sign up for after school?" I asked the others. I had already told the school newspaper I'd be on the staff again this year. Maybe do stage crew again too.

"Folk dancing," said Elizabeth. "I'm also going to be in a reading program for third graders, helping them one afternoon a week. That's credit toward the student service learning requirement."

Gwen said she was seriously considering music as a career—being a singer—either that or science. She was taking voice lessons, but she was also thinking about volunteering at the National Institute of Health. We looked at Pamela.

"Nothing," said Pamela.

"Nothing what?" I asked.

"I'm not going out for anything. My *mother* is my extracurricular activity. 'Mother: How to Avoid.'"

We were quiet a moment. What do you say to *that*? But Pamela suddenly thrust an imaginary glass in the air. "Let's *party!*" she said.

It was a warm breezy night, and we sprawled

around my room in our tank tops and drawstring bottoms. I brought up some chips and Cokes, and after we watched an old *Seinfeld* rerun, we talked about—what else?—boys.

"Have you heard from Joe?" I asked Gwen.

"Four e-mails," she said.

I looked at Elizabeth. "Ross?" I asked.

She grinned. "Two e-mails and a letter," she said. "A long letter."

"Hey!" I said.

Elizabeth rolled over on her back. "Is it true about Justin and Jill, do you think? What Karen's going around saying?"

"Don't believe anything Karen says," I told her. "She'll probably grow up to be a gossip columnist."

"But she says Jill told her that herself," said Elizabeth.

"Remember what Jill did in eighth grade, though," said Pamela. "She almost got Mr. Everett fired with that story that he came on to her."

"But what if it *is* true about Jill?" said Elizabeth. "Justin was kidding around with me over at Mark's the other day like maybe he wanted to go out again, but what if all this time he's been intimate with her?"

"*Intimate?*" we all exclaimed together.

"Who are you? Queen Victoria?" asked Pamela.

"You know what I mean," said Elizabeth.

"Well, maybe he wants to kiss one girl above the neck and another girl below," said Pamela.

"Oh, stop it," said Elizabeth. "But I don't really care, now that I've met Ross. I don't know when I'll see him again, but at least we can write. And who knows?"

"Absolutely!" I said. "Who knows? You may be assistant counselors there again next year."

Pamela and I were both smiling at Elizabeth like she was our little sister. It was so nice seeing her happy for a change. *We* were happy that Camp Overlook had been so good for her. I was proud of Pamela too, that she could back off the way she had. Maybe we *were* growing up. I thought back to the time Pamela bought her first bra. She had it in a little sack and was showing it to Elizabeth and me on the playground.

"Pamela," I said. "Do you remember when you were showing Liz and me your new Sears Ahh-Bra and Mark grabbed it out of your hands and went racing to the top of the monkey bars?"

We suddenly screeched with laughter and had to tell Gwen all about it. How we'd rushed off in a huff and refused to speak to the boys, and how they'd then gathered outside our window, calling for us to come out.

"The boys were *so* immature back then, weren't

they?" said Pamela. "I can't say that Mark has improved much. He and Legs have a lot in common, I think. You're lucky to be rid of him, Gwen."

"I know," said Gwen. "Especially since I met Joe."

"That was so weird, the way Legs just showed up at camp," said Elizabeth. "And to walk up just as you and Joe were kissing!"

"Yeah. Legs called the other night and wanted to know how serious I was about Joe. Said he *needed* me. His new girlfriend must have turned him down."

"What did you say?" I asked.

"What do you think, girl? I don't want to see *him*. You've got to be able to trust, and he proved I couldn't trust him. If I had it to do over, I wouldn't make the same mistake with Legs. I'd wait for someone I liked a whole lot more."

I quit massaging lotion into my feet and looked up. Was she saying what I *thought* she was saying?

Elizabeth stared at her too. "Wait to do *what*?" she asked breathlessly. Now even Pamela was staring. "You . . . you let him go all the way?"

"First base, second base, third base, the whole ball game," said Gwen.

We couldn't believe it. We were actually in the same room with a girl who had done IT? It was as though we expected Gwen to look different somehow. To metamorphose right in front of our eyes.

It was Elizabeth who broke the silence: "But . . . but you go to church!"

"So?" said Gwen.

"You sing in a *choir*!" Elizabeth gasped.

We couldn't help laughing. "And she's kind to her grandmother too, Elizabeth," I said.

But Elizabeth was still gawking at her. "Did you . . . like it?"

"Liz!" Pamela said, but we all wanted to know. I mean, it was one thing hearing it from my cousin Carol. It was another to hear it from one of us!

"Some of it," said Gwen, laughing a little. "We only did it four times. Maybe if we'd had a lot more time together, it would have been better."

"Gwen, you could have gotten pregnant!" I said, sounding like Elizabeth.

"Well, at least I had the good sense to be careful. 'No condom, no sex,' I told him. That's *one* thing I did right. I can't believe how naive I was, though." Gwen looked thoughtful. "He just seemed so *needy!* Like he was in *pain* he needed me so much—and that's sort of flattering. He's really not a bad guy, and I wanted to please him, but after meeting Joe, I realized how little Legs and I have in common."

I smiled at Gwen. "Everybody's angel, that's you. Your mom needed you, your grandmother needed you, your uncles, your aunts, your boyfriend. . . ."

"Where did you do it?" asked Elizabeth. She just wouldn't stop.

Gwen shrugged. "A picnic table at a roadside rest stop. The backseat of his car. His place, once, when no one was home."

"But . . . won't you be embarrassed when you see him around school?" Elizabeth asked. "I mean, he *knows* you down there, Gwen!"

Now we all burst out laughing.

"Well, only one more year to go," Gwen said. "He's a senior already; I won't have to see him around school after that."

Elizabeth stretched out on her back. "I don't think I'm going to have sex until I'm married," she declared. "I don't want to keep running into guys I've slept with. If other boys know you . . . *intimately*"—she emphasized the word this time, as though daring us to laugh at her—". . . I mean, don't you want to save something for your husband? Shouldn't there be something between you that's really special?"

It was something to think about. "Pledging to spend your lives together and take care of each other, maybe?" I suggested.

"There's more to marriage than sex, you know," said Gwen.

And I added, "Besides, it's different for mature men and women."

"Mature men and women!" Pamela exclaimed.

"Listen," I said, and recited the poem Dad had copied for Sylvia. I'd thought of it so often I'd memorized it by now:

> "O western wind, when wilt thou blow
> That the small rain down can rain?
> Christ, that my love were in my arms
> And I in my bed again!"

"Huh?" said Pamela.

"It doesn't rhyme," said Gwen.

"A-*gain*," I said, pronouncing the second syllable "*gane*." But when they still looked at me blankly, I changed the subject. I was ashamed of myself for repeating the poem that belonged to Dad and Sylvia. But I didn't tell them where I'd read it. That much I'd kept secret. And I promised myself that in the future, especially after Sylvia became my stepmom, I'd keep all these secrets to myself.

I thought everyone else went to sleep that night before I did. I couldn't get it out of my mind— Gwen and Legs. And what a jerk he was to tell Mark about it. Bragging, I'll bet.

At the same time I was remembering the day Patrick and I were alone in his house. We were down in the basement, and he was giving me a drum lesson. He stood behind me and put his arms around me to show how to hold the sticks . . . and then he was caressing my sides . . . up along my breasts. . . .

If his mom hadn't come home just then, would we have gone further than that? Did I want him to touch me there? Sure. It was *supposed* to feel good, wasn't it? Isn't that what sex is about?

"Alice," Elizabeth whispered. "What's the matter?" I didn't know she was awake.

"Nothing. Why?" I whispered back.

"You're restless."

"Sorry." I rolled over and faced her in the darkness. "I was thinking about Gwen," I said.

"Yeah. Me too. What do you think would happen if a man and woman fell in love but made an agreement not to touch each other until they were married?" she asked.

"Not at *all*?"

"Well, not their privates, anyway. I mean, if both of them—the man, too—came to marriage as pure and innocent as . . ."

". . . the driven snow," I said.

"Yeah."

"And then, on their wedding night, it was 'anything goes'?"

"Something like that."

"I don't know. I suppose they'd be exhausted from making up for lost time, or they'd have to get out a manual to see what goes where."

We both started to giggle.

"The comedians," said Gwen, startling us from her cot at the foot of the bed.

We shut up then and went to sleep.

# 17

# Celebration

One more week left before school. I looked at my dad one morning, his back to me as he fixed pancakes at the stove, and thought how he needed a night out. I'd been to camp, Lester was moving, and Dad hadn't even had a vacation. He had thought he would be married by now, back from his honeymoon, and here he was, cooking breakfast as usual.

"Dad," I said, "I'm taking you out to dinner tomorrow night. I've got it all planned." I didn't, but I'd take care of that in a hurry.

"Oh?" said Dad, turning. "What's the occasion?"

"You being my dad," I said.

"Well, that's a nice thought." He smiled. "I don't have to wear a tie, do I?"

"No. You always look good to me," I told him.

I took the Yellow Pages up to my room and

looked up restaurants. I scanned all the ads and came across a restaurant called Carmen's. *The Home of the Singing Waiters,* the ad read. I remembered how much fun I'd had when Lester took me to *Tony 'n' Tina's Wedding* for my birthday last May, so I called and made a reservation at Carmen's for Sunday night at seven, then checked to make sure I had enough money to cover our dinner. The following evening I gave Dad the address.

"Well!" he said as we pulled in the parking lot. "This is a new one! I don't think I've ever been here, Alice."

"Good!" I said, and hoped it wasn't a dump that served lousy food. The prices had been reasonable.

Once inside, I was relieved to find that it was clean and smelled delicious. Artificial grapevines covered the ceiling and ran down the walls in places, and all the waiters and waitresses were dressed like Italian peasants. A tall dark-haired man with a thin mustache came up to our table.

"Good *eve*-ning!" he said pleasantly. "I'm Francis, your waiter for tonight."

"Good *eve*-ning!" I said. "I'm Alice, and this is my dad." Dad smiled. So did Francis.

We listened to the day's specials, and after we'd each ordered, Francis returned from the kitchen with a basket of bread for our table. He was just about to walk away when I saw the piano player signal to him, and Francis stopped. Then, as the music started to play, Francis suddenly got down on one knee in front of me, arms outstretched, and sang "O Sole Mio." Dad listened delightedly, his face in a surprised smile.

Francis was handsome and had a great voice, and any girl in the restaurant would have been thrilled to have this hunk down on one knee in front of her. But I didn't know what I was supposed to do! Was this like in the movies, where a man and woman sing a duet and they have to stare into each other's eyes while they do it? Was it okay to look away? To blink? Was I supposed to ignore him and start eating or *what*?

I looked into his eyes until I felt my eyeballs go dry. It was just too embarrassing, so I dropped my eyes, but *then* I found myself staring at his *lap,* or what would have been his lap if he'd been sitting. No! I couldn't do that! I tried to think what a senior girl would do in a situation like this, and I sat demurely with my hands folded on the table. But then I realized that my napkin had fallen onto the floor, right on Francis's foot. Should I leave it there? Pick it up? Wait for Francis to pick it up? What did I do when the song was over? Tip him? *Kiss* him? *Why* had I brought my father to Carmen's?

Mercifully, the song was finished at last. Francis

got to his feet again, handed me my napkin, and gallantly kissed my hand, then went back to the kitchen.

"What a treat!" Dad said, reaching for the bread. "This was a nice surprise, Alice. I'll have to bring Sylvia here sometime."

I finally began to relax, because I figured nobody would serenade the same girl twice. It was fun now just watching. Every so often another waiter or waitress would stop serving and start singing—sometimes two or three of them together—and occasionally all the servers would join in the chorus, stopping whatever they were doing to sing. Several of the songs were in Italian, and it was great to see Dad enjoying himself so much.

"Oh, listen to this one!" he said when three men sang an aria from *Cosi Fan Tutte,* which, Dad told me, means "Women Are Like That."

Later, though, after we'd finished our salads and entrées, the most surprising thing happened. A waiter was serving at a table next to ours, and a waitress across the room, began singing to him in Italian.

Dad leaned forward. "Listen, Alice," he said. "This one is beautiful."

What is beautiful to my father, of course, sometimes sounds like noise to me, but then I'm tone-deaf, so that doesn't count. But because Dad loved the piece so much, I paid special attention. He was mouthing the words as the singers sang. It was obviously a duet, because the woman would sing a few measures and then the waiter would sing a few back to her. Dad sang softly along with the waiter.

And suddenly the waiter, noticing, bowed slightly and gestured toward Dad when it was his turn to sing next. The pianist waited. For just a moment Dad looked flustered; he hesitated, and then—to my astonishment—he rose to his feet and, with one hand extended toward the waitress, sang the baritone part. When it was the woman's turn, he didn't sit down, but waited while the waitress sang to him, smiling, and then he finished the piece with a flourish. His voice faltered a little on the high notes, but he brought it to a rousing end, and the whole room broke into applause. Some of the people at adjoining tables even stood up to clap for him. All the waiters and waitresses were smiling and applauding, and I don't think I ever saw Dad so pleased with himself when he sat back down again.

I could feel tears in my eyes. He was having such a good time! He needed times like these while Sylvia was away. I vowed that until she came back, I was going to take better care of my father.

I reached across the table and gave his arm a squeeze. "You were *wonderful*, Dad!" I said. "Wait till I tell Sylvia about this. You really surprised me!"

"Sometimes I even surprise myself," Dad said, beaming.

Lester had come in before we did and was up in his room, but I didn't describe our evening because I wanted to let Dad do the telling. I went up to the bathroom just as the phone rang. Dad was locking up for the night, so he picked up the phone in the hall downstairs.

"Sylvia!" he said when he answered, and I thought what a perfect time it was for her to call. I was tempted to lift the upstairs phone and tell her that Dad had been the hit of the evening, but I didn't dare.

I knew I should go on in the bathroom and close the door, but I always like to wait a minute or two when Sylvia calls to listen for Dad's response. I don't know why, I just have this feeling that . . . that after losing Mom . . . if Sylvia were to break their engagement, it would do my father in.

How did I know that her old boyfriend, Jim Sorringer, hadn't heard that Sylvia's sister was sick and had flown out to New Mexico to comfort Sylvia? If he could fly to England to surprise her, he could fly to Albuquerque. What if after Sylvia got out there, she decided that her sister needed her more than Dad did, and made up her mind to stay?

I leaned against the bathroom door, ready to duck inside if Dad looked up or Lester came out of his room.

There was a long pause from below, then a murmur, I couldn't make out what Dad was saying. But suddenly I heard, "Oh, Sylvia!"

I think I stopped breathing. I *know* I stopped breathing. My whole body grew rigid—waiting . . . waiting. . . .

And then he said, "Sweetheart, that's wonderful! That's the best news I've had all day. October it is, then. I'm so glad Nancy is doing well."

I danced silently around the hall upstairs. I waltzed into Lester's room, twirled around on his rug, and said, "Get ready to be best man in October, Lester!" And then, with Les still staring after me, I rushed downstairs, unable to control myself, threw my arms around Dad's middle, and gave him a bear hug. He just laughed and patted my head and went right on talking to Sylvia.

On Labor Day weekend Lester wanted to take some of his stuff over to the new apartment. "Okay," he said to me. "Call the Harpies and tell them they can help if they want."

I looked "Harpies" up in the dictionary. It said a Harpie was a creature in Greek mythology that is half woman, half bird. "Why do you call us Harpies?" I asked.

"Because you chatter like birds," said Lester.

"Then why don't you call us chicks or something?"

"Harpies are more you," he said.

I called Pamela first.

"You mean, *all* weekend? We can sleep over there and everything?" she asked excitedly.

I covered the phone with my hand and looked at Lester, who was drinking his coffee. "All weekend? she wants to know. Can we sleep over there too?"

Lester shot out a mouthful of coffee and coughed. He wiped his lips with one hand. "No, you're not staying all night. You can take your choice, tomorrow or Monday."

"Tomorrow," said Pamela when I told her.

"Tomorrow," Elizabeth agreed when I called.

"Okay," Lester said. "Tell them to be over here at ten o'clock, ready to work. We'll take some boxes over to the apartment and sort them there."

Pamela believes in dressing for success—we just have different definitions of "success"—and at ten on Sunday morning she arrived in short shorts. I mean, she didn't even have to bend over to show us her cheeks. She sported a halter top and thong sandals. Elizabeth, on the other hand, came over wearing the same jersey top she'd worn to mass that morning and had just pulled on a pair of cut-offs to go with it. I was in my usual jeans and T-shirt.

Elizabeth studied Pamela, who was stretching and giving an enormous yawn while we waited for Lester. "Why don't you just wear a sign saying FEEL ME?" she asked her.

Pamela glanced down at herself. "Why? What's the matter?"

"Those shorts!"

"If you got it, flaunt it," Pamela sang.

Lester came clattering downstairs carrying two boxes, one on top of the other.

"Well, this is a start," he said. "Good morning, ladies. Open the door for me, will you, Al?"

"Good mor-ning, Les-ter!" Pamela trilled.

He raised one eyebrow as he paused beside me at the screen. "Take my keys, would you, and open the trunk? I've got a couple more boxes upstairs."

We were soon rolling south on Georgia Avenue toward Takoma Park, and because it was a Sunday and a holiday weekend, the streets were deserted. Seven minutes later we were cruising down a tree-lined street of old Victorian houses, and thirty seconds after that Lester swung his car into the driveway of a large yellow house with brown trim and a wraparound porch.

"Oh, Lester!" I gasped. "You get to live *here*?"

"Isn't it great?" he said. "I still can't believe it." He turned off the motor. "Okay, everybody out, and carry something in with you. We take the stairs at the side of the house."

We headed for the separate entrance but bumped into each other because we kept stopping to exclaim over things: a huge sycamore with peeling bark, the two dormer windows at the front of the house, a little stone statue among the shrubbery, some old wicker furniture on the porch—a swing and a rocker.

"Come on up," Lester called, holding the door open with one elbow as he balanced a footlocker on his knee.

The apartment smelled of fresh paint, and the entryway was only half finished, but there was a stained-glass inset above a window on the opposite wall that let in the morning sun.

We put our boxes down and went exploring, excitedly commenting on every new detail we found. Lester tagged along, smiling broadly, pleased, I could tell, that we were so enthusiastic.

There were two large rooms with closets on one side of the hallway, two smaller rooms with closets on the other side. In between the smaller bedrooms was a sitting room with French doors that led out onto a screened porch.

"That's what was known as a sleeping porch at the turn of the century," Lester said. "Without air-conditioning, the kids—sometimes the whole family—would sleep on cots out on the porch in the summer. But see, if we open the French doors, it extends the living room so we can get more people in."

"Party, party, party!" Pamela cried. If I'd worried about Pamela being too subdued over the summer, it didn't seem I'd have to worry about that now.

Back inside, Lester pointed out the door that had been cut between the sitting room and one of the small bedrooms. The closet in that room had been removed and a kitchenette installed—a sink, a counter, a refrigerator, and a stove and oven.

"Not the best kitchen I've ever seen, but it'll do," Lester said.

"So who gets the two larger bedrooms, and who has to take the small one?" I asked.

"Paul and I get the big ones, and George gets the small one, because he's not sure he'll be here next summer. We might have to look for someone else."

"Boy, Lester, you are so lucky!" I said. I imagined

Elizabeth and Pamela and I sharing an apartment like this when we went to college. Sleeping out on a porch.

"Okay. Work time!" Lester said suddenly. "Here's what I want you to do. These are boxes of stuff I've had since grade school. Some of them, anyway. I want you to go through everything and sort them into three piles: stuff that looks like I should definitely keep, stuff you're not sure about, and stuff I could possibly throw away. I'll go through them after you decide, but this will make it easier. Got it?"

"Got it," said Elizabeth.

Lester went into his bedroom with some hardware and began adding more shelves to his closet.

We sat down on the floor, each of us with a box between her legs, and began. It was obvious Lester wasn't going to let us go through anything current—love letters from former girlfriends and stuff. But this would be interesting enough, we figured. Opening the first box, I found an odd assortment of stuff: an ashtray made of clay with Lester's initials on the bottom, a pin for perfect attendance, a flag, string, thumbtacks, a model jeep, scissors, wrapping paper, an old wallet. . . .

Elizabeth kept finding the most interesting stuff in her box. "Oh, m'gosh, his first-grade class picture!" she cried, and gave a little shriek. She showed us the photo with an arrow at the side pointing to a little boy with two missing teeth, grinning broadly. "Is that *Lester*?"

We howled and dug around some more. We could hear the tap of Lester's hammer back in his closet. I felt a little like a preschooler, having been given a box to entertain myself so I wouldn't get in the way.

"Having fun?" Lester called when he heard all the laughter.

"Oh, definitely!" said Elizabeth.

Lester wandered in to see what was so funny. He looked at the picture. "I was a real ladies' man, all right," he said, and went back to work.

Pamela seemed to have all Lester's school papers and notebooks. Every so often we'd hear her chuckle, and then she'd read something to us. But then we heard her say, "What's this?"

We watched her untape a yellowed piece of tablet paper, used as a wrapper around something else, it seemed. We stared in surprise as out fell a small pair of cotton underpants with lace around the legs.

Elizabeth clapped her hand over her mouth in amusement as we looked wide-eyed at each other.

"What does the paper say?" I asked.

Pamela turned it over. "It's just a spelling paper.

Looks like first or second grade with Lester's name at the top."

"What do you suppose . . . ?" Elizabeth said.

Suddenly Pamela took the underpants and pulled them over her head like a hat.

She motioned us to follow her and walked across the hall into Lester's bedroom.

"Boy, you find all kinds of stuff in boxes, don't you?" she said. "Ta da, Lester!"

Lester backed himself out of his closet and turned around. He stared at Pamela, then at her head, squinting slightly. "What's that?" he asked.

Pamela took the underpants off and read the label on the inside. "'Buster Brown, size 6,'" she said. "Hey, Les, you weren't a cross-dresser back in elementary school, were you?"

And suddenly, right before our eyes, Lester's face and neck and ears grew as pink as Elizabeth's jersey top. He reached out for the underpants, but Pamela snatched them away and held them behind her, eyes flashing mischievously. "Not until we hear the whole story, Les!" she said.

We hooted.

He laughed a little. "Some things were meant to stay private," he said.

That only made us more curious. "Tell us!" we begged.

He groaned and gave us a look. "Well, I was in second grade, and there was this little dark-haired girl named Maxine—Maxie, we called her—that I had a wild, secret crush on, and I was too shy to tell her."

"You? *Shy?*" cried Elizabeth.

"But not shy enough to take off her pants, huh?" teased Pamela.

Lester held up one hand.

"Go on," I said.

"One day on the playground Maxie jumped off the swings, and when she landed, she must have wet her pants. I didn't know what had happened at first, I just saw her jump and fall, and then she had this strange look on her face as she glanced around. A few minutes later, though, I was on the monkey bars and saw her go off behind the bushes in one corner and take off her underpants. She just left them there. When the bell rang, she came back and stood in line like everyone else, and I was the only one who knew she was naked under her dress."

"And you spent the afternoon trying to peek?" asked Pamela.

"No, no. But I kept thinking of her all afternoon, and when school was out, I went back there and got her underpants. They were wet, and there were ants all over them, but I took them home and rinsed them out. I was going to let them dry and then take them back to her the next day, but I was too embarrassed. So I never did. I kept them."

"Awwwwww!" we sang out together.

"She never knew?"

Lester shook his head. "Nope. One of the tragedies of second grade. And that's why I am what I am today."

"A lech?" asked Pamela.

"No! Hey!"

"A ladies' man," I said.

"Right," said Lester. "And now may I have Maxie's underpants, please?"

Pamela handed them over. "What are you going to do with them?" she asked.

"I don't know. I'd forgot all about them. But if ever there's a grade school reunion and I go back to Chicago and find Maxine, wouldn't it be something to walk up to her and say, 'For you, madame' and hand her the Buster Browns?" He stuffed them in one pocket.

"Ah! You never forget a first love," I said.

We went back to search for more of Lester's secrets, but that was the major find of the day.

Around two o'clock Lester went out to get some pizza for us. The minute he was gone, Pamela said, "I've got a great idea." She picked up the tissue paper that was in the first box and a pair of scissors, and while we watched, she made a life-size cutout of a pair of woman's underpants, scalloping the pant legs to look like lace. We grinned, puzzled. She cut out a bra next.

"What are you *doing*?" I asked.

"Watch," said Pamela. She took the ball of string and tied an end around an empty picture hanger on the wall of Lester's bedroom. Then she stretched it across the big window, cut it, and tied the other end around the hinge on his closet door. She took the pair of tissue panties and stapled them to the string, like clothes on a line. Then she stapled the bra. They blew slightly in the breeze.

We shrieked in delight and set to work cutting out more undies—panty hose, more underpants, another bra, a slip, even. By the time we heard Lester's car pull up again, there was a whole clothesline of women's tissue-paper undies fluttering in the breeze in front of Lester's window.

"You're a genius!" Elizabeth said to Pamela. "Oh, this is sweeeeet!"

"Break time!" Lester called, coming in the door. "Come and get it!" He took two boxes of pizza to the counter in the kitchen, and then, hearing us laughing in his bedroom, came to the doorway and stopped dead still. Suddenly he started to laugh.

"I see the Harpies are at it again," he said. "Very clever, girls, I must say."

We thought he'd rip them down, but he said, "George and Paul are coming by tomorrow with some of their stuff, and I think I'll leave it up, get a rise out of them."

We laughed some more.

"Of course, if Mr. Watts happens to check our apartment over the weekend, we could be out on our ear," Lester said. "But he may even want to borrow them for a while. Hang them up in his own window, get the neighbors talking."

We had a wonderful time!

After the first day of school I came home to find a cardboard box sitting on our porch addressed to me. The mail carrier had set it between the screen and the front door. There was a DEPARTMENT OF RECREATION sticker return address in the upper left corner, and all I could think of was that I probably left something behind at Camp Overlook and they'd finally traced it to me. Sneakers, maybe. But it wasn't heavy enough for sneakers. In fact, it hardly weighed anything at all. I sure hoped it wasn't dirty underwear. That would be so embarrassing!

I took it inside, set it on the kitchen table, and opened the flaps. It seemed to be full of shredded paper. I found an envelope, also from the Department of Recreation, with a letter inside from Connie Kendrick:

> Hi, Alice.
>
> We found this on the steps of the building last week when we came to work. There's a letter in it addressed to "Alice," and we decided that can only mean you. We're sending the whole thing exactly as we found it. Thanks for being part of our team this past summer. We loved having you.
>
> Connie

Was this a joke? I wondered. I couldn't see how there could be anything else in the box except paper. Then I found a grocery sack at the bottom, the top folded over. I opened it and lifted out a twig basket. Inside was a note on tablet paper:

Alice,

This for you Becaus that nite I was hiding in the tolet and you hug ⸻ I gess you like me a little too. ⸻ you decid to keep it maybe you ⸻ill think of me sometimes.

Latisha

# HAVE YOU READ ALL OF THE ALICE BOOKS?

## PHYLLIS REYNOLDS NAYLOR

STARTING WITH ALICE
Atheneum Books for
  Young Readers
  0-689-84395-X
Aladdin Paperbacks
  0-689-84396-8

ALICE IN BLUNDERLAND
Atheneum Books for
  Young Readers
  0-689-84397-6

LOVINGLY ALICE
Atheneum Books for
  Young Readers
  0-689-84399-2

THE AGONY OF ALICE
Atheneum Books for
  Young Readers
  0-689-31143-5
Aladdin Paperbacks
  0-689-81672-3

ALICE IN RAPTURE,
  SORT-OF
Atheneum Books for
  Young Readers
  0-689-31466-3
Aladdin Paperbacks
  0-689-81687-1

RELUCTANTLY ALICE
Atheneum Books for
  Young Readers
  0-689-31681-X
Aladdin Paperbacks
  0-689-81688-X

ALL BUT ALICE
Atheneum Books for
  Young Readers
  0-689-31773-5
Aladdin Paperbacks
  0-689-85044-1

ALICE IN APRIL
Atheneum Books for
  Young Readers
  0-689-31805-7
Aladdin Paperbacks
  0-689-81686-3

ALICE IN-BETWEEN
Atheneum Books for
  Young Readers
  0-689-31890-0
Aladdin Paperbacks
  0-689-81685-5

ALICE THE BRAVE
Atheneum Books for
  Young Readers
  0-689-80095-9
Aladdin Paperbacks
  0-689-80598-5

ALICE IN LACE
Atheneum Books for
  Young Readers
  0-689-80358-3
Aladdin Paperbacks
  0-689-80597-7

OUTRAGEOUSLY ALICE
Atheneum Books for
  Young Readers
  0-689-80354-0
Aladdin Paperbacks
  0-689-80596-9

ACHINGLY ALICE
Atheneum Books for
  Young Readers
  0-689-80533-9
Aladdin Paperbacks
  0-689-80595-0
Simon Pulse
  0-689-86396-9

ALICE ON THE OUTSIDE
Atheneum Books for
  Young Readers
  0-689-80359-1
Simon Pulse
  0-689-80594-2

GROOMING OF ALICE
Atheneum Books for
  Young Readers
  0-689-82
Simon
  0-68

ALICE
Atheneum
  Young Re
  0-689-82
Simon Puls
  0-689-85

SIMPLY ALICE
Atheneum Books
  Young Readers
  0-689-84751-3
Simon Pulse
  0-689-85965-1

PATIENTLY ALICE
Atheneum Books for
  Young Readers
  0-689-82636-2
Simon Pulse
  0-689-87073-6

INCLUDING ALICE
Atheneum Books for
  Young Readers
  0-689-82637-0